Stone Sighed And Closed His Eyes,

wondering how he could feel so contented in the presence of a woman who was supposed to be the enemy. This wasn't smart, he told himself. Letting her sneak under his defenses this way.

The truth was, he was entirely too close to falling under the spell of the very woman he'd been sent here to spy on.

He watched her stand up and place her glass beside his on the railing. That first description of her came back to him: "A perfectly awful woman.... A tramp named Lucy Dooley...."

The words echoed in his mind. *A tramp named Lucy Dooley... A tramp named Lucy Dooley...*

Who *was* Lucy Dooley?

What the hell was she doing out here?

And what the hell was he going to do about her?

Dear Reader,

We here at Silhouette Desire just couldn't resist bringing you another special theme month. Have you ever wondered what it is about our heroes that enables them to win the heroines' love? Of course, these men have undeniable sex appeal, and they have charm (loads of it!), and even if they're rough around the edges, you know that, deep down, they have tender hearts.

In a way, their magnetism, their charisma, is simply indescribable. These men are . . . simply Irresistible! This month, we think we've picked six heroes who are going to knock your socks off! And when these six irresistible men meet six *very* unattainable women, passion flares, sparks fly—and *you* get hours of reading pleasure!

And what month would be complete without a terrific *Man of the Month?* Delightful Dixie Browning has created a man to remember in Stone McCloud, the hero of *Lucy and the Stone. Man of the Month* fun just keeps on coming in upcoming months, with exciting love stories by Jackie Merritt, Joan Hohl, Barbara Boswell, Annette Broadrick, Lass Small and a *second* 1994 *Man of the Month* book by Ann Major.

So don't miss a single Silhouette Desire book! And, until next month, happy reading from . . .

Lucia Macro
Senior Editor

Please address questions and book requests to:
Reader Service
U.S.: P.O. Box 1325, Buffalo, NY 14269
Canadian: P.O. Box 1050, Niagara Falls, Ont. L2E 7G7

DIXIE BROWNING
LUCY AND THE STONE

SILHOUETTE *Desire*
Published by Silhouette Books
America's Publisher of Contemporary Romance

SILHOUETTE BOOKS

ISBN 0-373-05853-5

LUCY AND THE STONE

DIXIE BROWNING

has written over fifty books for Silhouette since 1980. She is a charter member of the Romance Writers of America and an award-winning author, and she has toured extensively for Silhouette Books. Dixie also writes historical romances with her sister under the name Bronwyn Williams.

This book is dedicated to two writers' groups that provided great ideas and even greater hospitality: First, my daughter Sarah and her fifth-grade class at the University School. And second, Peg McCool and her Friday critique group in Tacoma—Carol, Micky, Mary, Melinda and Anita...and Charlie, of course. Many thanks!

Prologue

He caught the phone on the fifth ring, breathing heavily, swearing silently. "Yeah, McCloud here!"

"John Stone, is that you?" Aunt Alice. Alice Hardisson was the only person in the world who called him John Stone.

"How are you, Aunt Alice? It's been a long time."

"I'm right well, thank you. I understand you were in the hospital. I hope you're feelin' better now." The quiet, well-bred Southern voice waited politely for him to fill her in on all the pertinent details.

Now, how the hell could she have known that? Other than the occasional family funeral, when he happened to be in the country, and the basket of jams and jellies she ordered sent to his mail drop every year at Christmas, there had been little contact between them for years.

Unless there'd been something in the news. He'd been in no condition to know or care at the time. "I'm fine, Aunt Alice. Or as fine as a man can be after overdosing on hospital food. How's Liam? Still hunting rabbits on his day off?" Liam was the Hardissons' butler. He was seventy-five if he was a day, and he'd been Stone's mainstay in the years he had spent in the old Hardisson mansion after his parents had been killed.

"Liam's retired now. Mellie died last year, and I thought it best to let him spend his last days with his grandchildren."

Best for whom, Aunt Alice? Stone thought wryly. Despite the code of noblesse oblige that was bred into the bones of women like Alice Hardisson, his aunt seldom put herself out to any great extent for any interest but her own. Unless it was for her only child.

Stone himself was a case in point. His mother and Alice had been sisters. Stone's parents had been killed by a drunk driver when he was six and a half years old, and Alice had taken him in. Noblesse oblige. Her own son, his cousin Billy, had been five then.

But while Alice, accompanied occassionally by Billy and his nanny, had traveled to Scotland for the salmon fishing, to Paris for the fashion hunting or to some spa in Arizona twice a year for whatever benefits she derived there, Stone had invariably been left with Liam and Mellie.

Noblesse oblige. Take in needy kinfolk, put food in their mouths, a roof over their heads and inquire graciously once or twice a year to be sure there's nothing more they need.

And as soon as they're weaned, pack them off to boarding school.

"Are you in town, Aunt Alice?" Stone asked, hoping she wasn't.

"No, I'm still down here in Atlanna."

She always called it Atlanna. With her gentle, unconscious arrogance, she probably spelled it that way.

"How's Billy? Still thinking about making a run for the senate one of these days?"

"Well now, that's what I called you about, John Stone. I reckon you heard Billy got hisself mixed up with this perfectly awful woman a while back and ended up married to her."

Stone lowered himself carefully onto the sofa and tucked the phone against his neck. "I seem to remember seeing an announcement."

"I had Ella Louise mail out announcements so it wouldn't look like such a hole-in-the-wall affair, but I knew it wouldn't last. Naturally, I made the best of it for Billy's sake, but she just wasn't Our Kind of People."

Stone smiled grimly. Very few people made Alice's list of Our Kind of People. He himself had certainly fallen far short, despite their kinship.

"I took her in hand for poor Billy's sake. The girl had no more sense of how to go on than a stray cat. All that hair, and those cheap clothes! Naturally I did my best to show her how to dress and speak and how to act around decent folk without embarrassing herself."

Without embarrassing Alice Hardisson, Stone interpreted, making a noncommittal murmur. Alice would be the mother-in-law from hell, no matter who Billy married. Stone could almost find it in his heart to be sorry for the poor girl, but then, any female with no more sense than to marry Bill Hardisson probably deserved what she got.

He picked up the monologue still in progress. "Been hearin' these awful rumors. Nothing in the papers yet, thank goodness, but I'm afraid she's out to make mischief. I can't think of anyone else who would do such a thing." She sighed. "John Stone, I'm worried."

"Why'd he marry her? Was she pregnant?"

"Good heavens, certainly not! Billy has better sense than to get hisself involved with a tramp like Lucy Dooley!"

"I thought you said he married her. That's about as involved as you can get."

"He's just too trustin' for his own good. Poor Billy. When a flashy tramp like that Dooley woman keeps flauntin' herself at the club pool, wearin' little more than she came into the world with—"

"That's where he met her? The club?"

"That's what I said, didn't I? Oh, I'll admit the girl has a common type of looks that men seem to like—she certainly took my poor boy in, but before they'd even been married six months, she showed her true colors. Poor Billy, he pleaded with her to behave herself. But when she started carryin' on in front of all their friends—why, he had to ask her to leave."

"They're divorced now, I take it. So what's the problem?"

"Well, naturally he divorced her. At least she had the decency to leave town, but we're afraid now that he's runnin' for the state senate, she'll come back and cause trouble."

"Why?"

"Well, for goodness' sake, John Stone, for money! What else would her kind want?"

"You mean that flock of tame lawyers you keep on a leash didn't sew her fingers together before they let Billy marry her?"

"I was out of the country at the time, and that girl had poor Billy so besotted he just up and married her without makin' her sign doodlysquat! Lord knows what she threatened to do, but he ended up paying her two hundred thousand dollars a year for three years just to stay out of Georgia. Poor Billy, he's always been too soft-hearted for his own good."

Or too softheaded. Six hundred thousand was a lot of loot!

"Now that the payments have ended, we're afraid she's goin' to try and get more by threatenin' to go to the papers with her vicious lies. She knows good and well he's lookin' to go to Washin'ton after one or two terms in Atlanna. That's just the sort of thing her kind would do. Like all those hussies who end up on the television by threatenin' decent men in high places. You know who I mean, John Stone?"

"I seem to recall a few such incidents, but why would you—"

"I just told you—there are already rumors circulatin' around town. They can't have come from any other source, because everybody here loves Billy. He's always been a good boy."

Stone grimaced. Billy loved Billy. Aunt Alice loved Billy. The rest of the world probably knew him for what he was—the spoiled, immature product of privilege and neglect. Not for the first time, Stone was glad he'd broken with the family at the age of fourteen, when he'd been shipped off to military school, and that it had never been "convenient" for him to spend much time with his aunt after that.

"Exactly what is it you think I can do?" he asked.

She didn't beat around the bush. "I understand you've been hurt right bad, and you're goin' to be laid up for a while. I thought you might like to—"

"You thought I might like to go down to Atlanta and take her out for you?"

"What? Don't be foolish, John Stone. If you want to take her out, that's your concern, but I warn you, she's not Our Kind of People."

"I didn't mean— That is, take her out means—" He gave up. He spoke three languages fluently and got by in a couple more. He had never spoken his aunt's language, and probably never would.

"It just so happens that I've arranged for this woman to spend the summer at a place called Coronoke—it's a little speck of an island off the North Carolina coast. I understand there aren't any telephones there, and certainly no reporters, so I thought if you could go along and kind of keep an eye on her, just make sure she doesn't get up to any more mischief—"

"Whoa! Aunt Alice, I don't even know this woman, and you want me to be her jailer?"

"Don't raise your voice to me, John Stone. I didn't say that. All I ask is that you go down there and take advantage of the cottage I've leased in your name. You don't have to let her know who you are—in fact, it's probably better if you don't—but you can keep her entertained so she'll forget about causin' trouble for Billy, at least until after his weddin'."

"His *wedding?*"

"Oh. Did I forget to mention that Billy's gettin' married again in August? This lovely girl—she's the granddaughter of old Senator Houghton—"

"In other words, you want me to pen this woman up on a deserted island— What did you call it?"

"Coronoke, and it's certainly not deserted."

"Right. Pen her up, don't let her near a phone, and if she makes any suspicious moves, sic the *federales* on her, right?"

By the time he finished, Alice had very politely hung up on him. Feeling worse than he had when he'd come out of the hospital five days earlier, Stone called her back and, after apologizing, found himself reluctantly agreeing to finish up his recuperation on the island of Coronoke.

And, incidentally, to do his best to distract the greedy little hustler who was out to ruin Billy's chances for marital happiness and political success.

Actually, he'd sort of had other plans, but . . .

"How'd you find out I'd been in the hospital, Aunt Alice?"

"Carrie Lee Hunsucker's great nephew works for the *Constitution*. Carrie Lee belongs to the Wednesday Morning Music Club."

And he'd thought *he* had contacts.

"I'm doing this partly for your sake, John Stone, because I understand you don't even have a decent place to live. This way, you can just lie around until you're feelin' well enough to go back to work doin' whatever it is you do these days."

Whatever it was he did. As if she didn't know. Why else had she tracked him down and sicced him on some bimbo who was out to ruin her son's political career before it even got off the ground? Which just might, incidentally, be the best thing that could happen to the state of Georgia.

On the other hand, he did need a vacation. Gazing around at the hotel room he had taken when he'd left the hospital, Stone compared it to a cottage on a small island somewhere down South. The room was about average for a residential hotel. He'd bunked in far worse, under far worse conditions, but now that he thought about it, soaking up the sun on a private beach didn't sound half bad, either.

"I guess I can do that," he'd said finally, adding a halfhearted thanks.

"You don't have to thank me, John Stone. It's the least I can do for my own sister's boy."

Stone hung up the phone with the uncomfortable feeling that he'd just been hooked, gaffed and landed.

Noblesse oblige.

One

The first day belonged to Stone, and he was determined not to waste a single salt-cured, sun-soaked minute of it. By tomorrow the Dooley woman would probably be here. Which meant his baby-sitting duties would begin. But for now there was nothing to keep him from lying on an inflated inner tube, his naked feet dangling in the cool waters of Pamlico Sound, while a half-empty beer bottle rested on the bright pink scar on his belly.

Coronoke. Translated, it had to mean paradise. Stone had never heard of the place. It wasn't even on the map! But now that he'd discovered it, he fully intended to spend some serious downtime here. Inhaling, exhaling—quietly growing moss on his north side.

Not to mention keeping the Dooley woman from embarrassing his aunt and bleeding her dry. As far as Stone was concerned, Billy could clean up his own messes, but Billy wasn't the only one who stood to get hurt this time.

Women of his aunt's generation were poorly equipped to deal with the tabloid press and sleaze TV. It would kill her to have the Hardisson name dragged through that kind of mire. If it was in his power to prevent it, he would.

Saltwater dried on his shoulders, and he flexed them, liking the contrast between the sun's heat and the water's coolness. Liking the feeling of utter and complete relaxation that had begun seeping into his bones even before he'd checked into his cottage, stashed his gear and stepped out of his shoes.

Stone was an accredited journalist. Affiliated for the past nine years with IPA, he had covered most of the major conflicts and natural disasters around the globe. Although he tried to avoid political campaigns—most of which were natural disasters of major proportions. A guy had to draw the line somewhere.

He'd been covering a humanitarian aid convoy in East Africa when a stray bullet from a sniper's gun had struck the gas tank of the vehicle he was riding in. His photographer had been killed outright in the explosion. His driver, who'd been thrown clear, had broken his little finger. Stone ended up with a severe concussion, several broken ribs, a torn lung and an assortment of scrap steel embedded in various parts of his anatomy.

He'd been incredibly lucky. He could have ended up spread over several acres of desert. Instead, here he was a few months later, armed with nothing more lethal than a pair of binoculars and a birding guide, floating around on an inner tube, soaking up Carolina sunshine and watching a squadron of pelicans flap past.

At least, he thought they were pelicans. He was going to have to bone up on his Audubon if he didn't want to blow his cover. He'd considered bringing along his laptop to work on the series of articles he'd been doing on spec. One of the major syndicates had put out a few feelers after his series on archaeological piracy, and he'd been flattered . . . and interested.

At the last minute he'd decided against it. He wasn't ready to go back to work. His brain was still lagging about two beats behind his body, possibly because he hadn't had a real vacation in more years than he could remember.

Or possibly because he'd come so damned close to checking out permanently, he'd been forced to face up to what his life had become.

Which was empty. No ties, no commitments, nothing to show for his thirty-seven years other than a few yellowed scrapbooks and a few awards packed away in storage with his old tennis racquet.

In that frame of mind, he had impulsively put a call through to a guy he hadn't heard from in over a year. Reece was the brother of the woman Stone had almost married once upon a time. A woman who'd finally had the good sense to marry some decent nine-to-fiver who had offered her the home and kids she wanted. Stone had lost touch with Shirley Stocks, but from time to time he still heard from her brother. The kid had thought Stone was some kind of hero, always flying off to the world's hot spots at a moment's notice.

Reece was currently studying journalism at UNC. As it appeared that Stone would soon be headed south to the Old North State, it had seemed like a good opportunity to get together.

Bird-watching! Thank God Reece didn't know the depths to which his hero had sunk. It had been his aunt's idea, the bird-watching cover. Evidently she'd mentioned it when she'd reserved the cottage for the summer, and the real estate agent had mailed him a bundle of birding data along with directions for finding the place. Rather than bother to explain that he didn't know a hummingbird from a hammerlock, and couldn't care less, he'd let it stand. But this whole drill was beginning to strike him as slightly bizarre. Not to mention slightly distasteful.

Reluctantly, Stone began paddling himself back to shore. His shoulders, his thighs and his belly were starting to tingle. Sun had never been a particular problem before, but a few months of holding down a hospital bed had a way of thinning a guy's skin right down to the nerve endings.

The cottage wasn't luxurious, but it was comfortable. Better yet, it was quiet. Best of all, it was his alone for the next two months—books on the shelf, cigarette burn on the pine table, rust-stained bathtub and all.

All it lacked was a Home Sweet Home sampler nailed to the wall. He'd already taken the liberty of rearranging some of the furniture and was considering dragging a cedar chaise longue into the living room from the deck, just because he liked the way it smelled.

Home sweet home. Maybe it was time he thought about getting himself something more permanent than a mail drop, a storage shed and a series of hotel rooms. The last real home he could remember—and the memory was fading like a cheap postcard—was a white frame house with a wraparound porch and three pecan trees in the backyard that were home to several platoons of squirrels.

Decatur, Georgia. They had moved there when his father had gotten a promotion, just in time for Stone to enter the first grade. Before the year was out, that portion of his life had come to an abrupt end.

As for the Hardissons' Buckhead mansion, the only time he had felt at home there had been when his aunt was off on one of her jaunts and Mellie had let him eat in the kitchen with the help. He could still remember sitting on an overturned dishpan in a chair and stuffing himself with her Brunswick stew and blackberry dumplings.

Jeez! When was the last time he'd thought of all that? This was what happened when a guy had too much time on his hands, Stone told himself. Ancient history had never been his bag.

After making himself a couple of sardine sandwiches and forking his fingers around a cold beer, he wandered out onto the screened deck. Still wearing his trunks, he took a hefty bite of sandwich and turned his thoughts to his unlikely assignment. He'd been in the hospital when Billy had won the primary last month, else he might have heard something. Not that Georgia politicians were of any great interest at IPA. At least, not since the Carter days.

Senator Billy?

God, the mind boggled. Stone hadn't seen his cousin since their great-uncle Chauncey Stone's funeral in Calhoun, several years ago. Billy had been flushed and smelling of bourbon at eleven in the morning. He had escorted his mother into the church, but Stone had seen the bimbo waiting in his red Corvette farther down the street.

Family. Funny how it could influence you in ways you never even suspected. He didn't particularly like his cousin. He didn't know if he loved his aunt or not, but he'd always recognized her strength, and strength was something Stone had been taught to admire. Strength of character. Strength of purpose. His aunt had both. And when he thought about her at all, he admired her for what she was, and didn't dwell too long on what she wasn't.

Sipping his beer, Stone let his mind wander unfettered across the tapestry of the past thirty-seven years. After a while the empty bottle slipped to the floor and he began to snore softly in counterpoint to the cheerful sound of screeching gulls, scolding crows and gently lapping water.

Lucy watched the odometer roll over a major milestone. She flexed her arms one at a time, then flexed her tired back and wondered how far it was to the next rest area. She'd been driving for eight solid hours, stopping only for gas and junk food, and to wolf down a bacon cheeseburger and a large diet drink for lunch. By the time she'd gotten as far as Kernersville, she was already having second thoughts, but it was too late to turn back, even if she'd wanted to. Her gas was turned off, her mail and paper deliveries stopped.

Alice Hardisson didn't owe her a thing. Lucy knew she should have had more pride than to accept the offer, but one didn't argue with a Hardisson. Not argue and win, at any rate. Fortunately, she had learned early on to be a gracious loser. Or, at the very least, to know when the game was lost.

And the game *was* lost. Alice had won. Surrendering to the inevitable, Lucy vowed to enjoy every minute of her unexpected free vacation, and if that made her a parasite, she'd just have to grin and bear it. She couldn't even remember the last vacation she had taken. Her honeymoon trip with Billy didn't count. That had been a revelation, not a vacation.

Guiltily, she knew she was looking forward to it, too. A whole summer of swimming, sleeping late, staying up all night to read all those juicy escapist books she never had time to read during the school year.

And no more frozen dinners. No more school cafeteria! She was going to eat fried corned-beef hash with catsup and onions for breakfast and fried banana sandwiches for supper, and work off all the calories by walking and swimming.

Who said you can't have it all?

What's more, she was going to play her guitar until she built up a set of calluses that would shatter bricks. And she'd sing along, even if she couldn't carry a tune. Which she couldn't.

The night Alice had called, Lucy had been feeling mildewy. Rain always depressed her, and it had been raining for over a week. Studying the help-wanted ads for a summer job hadn't improved her mood, either.

When she'd picked up the phone, expecting to hear Frank's familiar voice, and heard Alice Hardisson's instead, she'd been so shocked she inhaled a piece of popcorn. It was minutes before she could speak coherently. Even now she wasn't sure she'd been thinking coherently. "Goodness, you're the last person in the world I ever expected to hear from," she'd managed to say.

They had been friends while Lucy was married to Billy, or at least as much as two women of different generations and totally different backgrounds could ever be friends. Alice had been quietly furious about the marriage, but she'd covered it well. Every inch the gracious lady, she had never let on by so much as a single cross word. Instead, she'd had her secretary mail out announcements and then hustled Lucy off to do some se-

rious shopping, tactfully avoiding comment on the
flowing shirts and tight pants she'd favored back then.

Alice *always* wore dresses. Gradually Lucy had begun
to notice that her clothes never looked quite new—never
looked quite fashionable, either—yet they never looked
really *un*fashionable. Understatement, she came to learn,
was a fashion statement all its own.

She also learned that Alice's particular brand of understatement could cost a mint.

She had learned much more than that from Mother
Hardisson. Gradually she had come to admire the
woman, emulating the way she dressed, the way she ex-
pressed herself—even the way she smiled.

Grins were vulgar, loud laughter quite beyond the pale.

Lucy hadn't even known what a pale was.

But by the time she had learned to cover her five-foot-
eleven, one-hundred-forty-pound frame in suitably un-
derstated fashions, to wear modest pearl buttons in her
ears instead of three-inch gold-plated hoops with dan-
gles and to drink watery iced tea instead of diet cola with
her meals, her marriage was already foundering.

By the time Alice had left for Scotland, Lucy had been
wondering how long she could go on hiding the truth
about the wretched state of affairs at 11 Tennis Court
Road. Billy began drinking soon after breakfast, and
when he drank, he was mean. Lucy had tried repeatedly
to make him seek help, which had only made him
meaner.

Alice had gone from Scotland to France and then directly back to Scotland, almost as if she didn't want to
come home. Lucy could have used her support at the
time—particularly after she lost the baby. But Alice
would have been devastated, and Lucy couldn't wish that

for her. Alice had still been visiting friends abroad when the divorce had become final.

It had been a quick one. At least Billy had agreed to that much, paying for her requisite six weeks' residency. Afterwards, Lucy had sold her wedding and engagement rings, and the diamond and sapphire guard ring Billy had given her for her birthday, a week after their wedding, for enough to relocate. She'd been intending to try Richmond, but she'd missed a turnoff and ended up taking I-40 through Winston-Salem. Just north of town, her car had broken down, and by the time she'd had it repaired, she had only enough money left to rent a cheap room and look for a job. It was a way of life which was all too familiar. Unscheduled moves, unscheduled stops.

But the job had turned out to be a good one, waitressing at a popular restaurant. She'd attended night school, finished her teaching degree and was now in her second year of teaching sixth grade. Not half bad under the circumstances, she thought proudly.

"Lucy, my dear," Alice had said that rainy night nearly two weeks ago. "Why didn't you ever write? You knew I'd be concerned."

"I'm sorry, Mother Hardisson" was all Lucy could think of to say. *Sorry your son turned out to be such a bastard, sorry he robbed you of your grandchild and sorry you can't divorce him, too. You'd be better off, believe me!*

"Oh, please, my dear. I'm the one who's sorry I wasn't here when you needed me. I'm sure if I'd been able to reason with you both, we could have worked things out. Now I reckon it's too late."

It had been too late the first time Billy had struck her. It had been too late the first time he'd brought one of his floozies home and she had found them in the hot tub together, jaybird-naked.

It had been over the day she found his private stash in the celadon vase on the mantel. She had flushed it down the john and threatened to tell his mother if he didn't straighten out. Wild with anger, he had struck her on the side of the head, knocking her halfway down the stairs. A few hours later she had miscarried.

But Lucy hadn't said any of that. It wasn't the sort of thing one said to a woman like Alice Hardisson. Billy's mother had always been kind to her, even though Lucy knew she'd been shocked right down to her patrician toenails when her precious son had run off and married a nobody who'd been migrating north from Mobile, Alabama—a part-time student, part-time lifeguard, with no more background than a swamp rat.

Alice had graciously refrained from offering to buy her off. Instead, she had made the best of her son's unfortunate marriage, and Lucy would always love her for that. Her father hadn't left her much—a battered old twelve-string and a lot of wonderful memories—but he had left her a legacy of pride.

When, after three years, her ex-mother-in-law had called to tell her about the cottage she had leased for her companion, Ella Louise, to vacation in while Alice went on a two-month cruise with friends, Lucy's first impulse had been to hang up.

But then Alice had gone on to tell her about Ella Louise's tripping over a dog and breaking her hip. "Naturally, a place like that would be out of the question. She's gone to stay with her sister down in some little town in Florida. So you see, if you don't take the cottage, it will just go to waste. It was too late to cancel by the time I thought about it."

"But why me? My goodness, surely you know someone else who would like to use it."

"My dear child, you must allow me to soothe my conscience by providin' you with a little vacation, else I'll
never forgive myself for bein' away when you needed me
most."

And so Lucy, having been taught by the grande dame
herself, had graciously allowed herself to be persuaded.
There was no real reason why she shouldn't accept a gift
from a friend, she rationalized. The friend could afford
it, and obviously wanted to do it. Why else had she gone
to the trouble of tracking her down after all this time?

Come to think of it, how *had* she tracked her down? A
forwarding address? Medical records?

Lucy was too tired even to wonder about it now. And
too hot. Her backside was permanently bonded to the
vinyl seat cover of her car. At least she was a whole lot
closer to the end of her journey than when she had set out
this morning shortly after daybreak.

Frank had risen early and come over to help her load
the car. He'd promised to water her plants and air her
apartment when and if the rain ever stopped. She had
hugged his two daughters, one of whom was her student, and then hugged Frank, avoiding the question in his
eyes the same way she had been avoiding it all year.

She didn't love Frank Beane. Liked him enormously,
adored his motherless children, but as much as she longed
for a home and a family, she wasn't about to take another chance. She had excellent taste in friends, lousy
taste in husbands, but at least she had sense enough to
learn from her mistakes.

Reaching over, Lucy patted the scuffed hard-shell case
that held Pawpaw's old twelve-string. She had strapped

it into the passenger seat with the seat belt, having filled the back seat with books, linens, clothes and groceries.

"One of these days, Pawpaw, I'll have music on my own back porch and a garden full of okra and tomatoes for gumbo, and maybe even a few cats. One of these days..."

She sighed. Lucy had no use for nostalgia. It was a nonproductive exercise, brought on, no doubt, by smelling salt air again after all these years. This was different from the Gulf Coast, but salt air was salt air, and Lucy was tired.

Pawpaw had been a roughneck. He had worked the oil fields, moving from place to place, but never too far from the Gulf Coast. Lucy, motherless for as long as she could recall, could remember piling into what they used to call the Dooley Trolley, an old camper truck held together with duct tape and baling wire, and setting out in the middle of the night for a new job, a new town—new friends.

Lucy could barely remember her mother, but there'd always been women in her life. Pawpaw—tanned and handsome, with his black-dyed hair and his broad grin, the metallic scent of crude oil that clung to his clothes, usually tempered by a mixture of sweat, bourbon and bay rum—had been like a magnet to women. A good-looking, good-natured man, Clarence Dooley's only weakness had been an itchy foot and a deep-seated aversion to long-term commitment.

Nearing the tall, spiral-striped lighthouse, where the highway turned west, Lucy squinted against the glare of afternoon sun and thought about Pawpaw and Ollie Mae, one of Pawpaw's lady friends, sitting on the back stoop after supper, Pawpaw playing his guitar and singing, and Ollie Mae sawing away at her fiddle, the sagging flesh of her upper arm swaying in time with each stroke. Pawpaw had been dead nearly eighteen years now, and Lucy had long since lost track of Ollie Mae and Lillian and the rest of Clarence Dooley's mistresses.

For one isolated moment she felt utterly alone. And then she shrugged and put it down to no more than being in a strange place, among strangers. Something she should be used to by now.

It would pass. Everything passed, good and bad.

"You'll like Maudie and Rich," said Jerry, the boy from the marina where Lucy had been instructed to leave her car and take a boat out to Coronoke. "Maudie—she's my cousin on my mother's side. Well, I reckon if you go back a little ways, on my daddy's side, too. She used to be—Maudie, that is—she used to caretake over to Coronoke, but then this guy—"

Lucy clutched her guitar case in both arms, wondering if there was going to be much spray. She'd brought her raincoat, but like an idiot, she'd left it in the trunk of her car.

Watch where you're going! she wanted to say, but didn't because he was only a boy. Still, she'd feel a whole lot safer if he would keep his mind on what he was doing instead of staring at her as if she were some kind of freak and filling her in on the pedigree of people she had never heard of and would probably never meet.

There was no spray. In fact, they were barely making a wake. Lucy could have swum faster than this if she hadn't been so blessed tired. The boy—he couldn't be more than sixteen or so—was looking at her in a certain way that made her feel like the butterfat champion at the county fair.

After thirty-four years she ought to be used to it. Towering over everyone in sight, having men make lewd propositions without even getting to know her first. It was all part of the curse that had befallen her at the age of twelve, when she'd shot up to five feet eight and her breasts had burst out of her training bra.

"Sugar, there's not a blessed thing you can do about it, less'n you was to get fat as a sausage all over," her father's lady friend, Lillian, had told her. "Even then, it prob'ly wouldn't do you no good. Girls with your looks's got a hard row to hoe, and being big just makes you stand out more." Lillian had been one of Lucy's favorites. A blowsy redhead, she'd been kind enough to take a motherly interest in Lucy at a time when Lucy was undergoing a lot of frightening changes in her body and in her emotions.

"Don't you never let a boy lay a hand on you, you hear me? They'll try. Lord knows they'll try to make you think they're a-hurtin' somethin' fierce and you're their only hope o' salvation. But you tell 'em you got the curse real bad, and your Pawpaw just sent you out to get some gun oil, 'cause he's a-cleaning up his shotgun. If that don't shrivel up what ails 'em, you use your knee where it'll do the most good, y'hear?"

Lucy sighed. Nostalgia. It had to be the smell of all this salt air. She'd never been one for looking back. "Big adventures ahead, li'l sugar," Pawpaw always used to say when they'd load up the trolley and light out in the middle of the night for a new town, a new job. "That ol' highway's unrollin' right in front of your pretty brown eyes. You just keep on a-lookin' straight ahead."

The narrow beach was striped with coral sunlight and lavender shadows when Jerry pulled up to the pier on Coronoke. He clanged the tarnished brass bell that was attached to the side of a shed and within minutes, a woman came jogging down through the woods.

"Hi, you must be Mrs. Dooley. I'm Maudie Keegan."

"It's *Ms.* That is, I was married, but I took back my own name so—"

"I know what you mean. Neither fish nor fowl. Me, either, until I solved my problem by becoming Mrs. Keegan."

By which Lucy concluded that Maudie Keegan had been married before and had shed her first husband's name at the same time she'd shed him.

Lucy had gone from Dooley to Hardisson and back to Dooley so fast, even the IRS had trouble keeping up with her. She only hoped her social security would make it through the maze by the time she was old enough to need it.

"I see you stocked up on canned things. Good." Maudie reached for the box of groceries Jerry was lifting out, and the three of them relayed everything up from the pier, along a winding path through shadowy, fragrant woods, to a small cottage perched a hundred-odd feet from the edge of the sound.

"Is that it?" Maudie Keegan asked when the last of the load was transported. "Okay, then here's the rundown. Your closest neighbor is a birder named McCloud. He'll be here all summer. There's a novelist installed in Blackbeard's Hole, but you won't see much of him. He comes every year and holes up until Labor Day, working on the Great American Novel. There's a couple from Michigan due in tomorrow and two family groups coming the next weekend. Eventually you'll probably meet everybody, but no one's obliged to socialize. Rich and I are on the other side of the island in the old lodge."

Her small hands moved constantly while she spoke, and Lucy watched, mesmerized, murmuring an appropriate response when necessary.

"One of us will pick up mail and messages every day or so, and we have a radio for emergencies. The boats at the pier are for the guests. When we're full up, we sign up a day in advance so everyone can make plans accordingly, but when there're only a few people in residence, feel free to take one out. Rich keeps them fueled up. Meanwhile, if you need anything at all, one of us is usually available. Just follow the trail around the island until you come to a place that looks as if it ought to be condemned. That's ours."

Bemused, Lucy watched the woman jog through the woods until the lengthening shadows swallowed her up. Turning, she met an all-too-familiar look in the eyes of the young man from the marina.

Evidently, Jerry appreciated king-size blondes with brown eyes, wild hair and big mouths.

She sighed, knowing she would have to make certain things clear to avoid any future misunderstanding. Lucy got along well with people of all ages and sexes, but with the male variety, she had long since learned to get across a subtle message right from the first.

Accessible she was; available she was not.

Two

Stone, once more half-asleep on a drifting inner tube, roused at the sound of voices. Evidently, Lucy Dooley had emerged from her cottage. La Dooley, as he had taken to calling her in his mind. The ex-Mrs. William Carruthers Hardisson.

His quarry, he thought reluctantly.

She had arrived late the previous evening. Stone had heard the sound of an outboard from the screened deck of his own cottage. A few minutes later, he'd seen Maudie Keegan emerge from the woods, followed by the kid from the marina and a tall, shaggy-haired blonde, all carrying boxes, bags and baggage.

Alice hadn't told him what she looked like, only that she had a common type of prettiness that appealed to some men. Evidently, it had appealed to Billy. The woman had waited until Alice was conveniently out of the way before she'd put the moves on poor Billy.

Poor Billy? Hell, now he was starting to sound like Alice!

Stone had considered wandering over to meet his new neighbor last evening. He'd decided against it. She wasn't going to do anything the first day or so. Maybe not at all. And as long as she behaved herself, she wouldn't even have to know he was there.

He continued to watch her from a safe distance, feeling pleasantly relaxed after a half hour spent walking the sandy perimeter of the island. Idly he wondered, without putting any great degree of effort into it, what a woman of her sort was doing coming out to a nowhere place like Coronoke. If her plan was to blackmail the Hardissons now that her ex-husband was in a particularly vulnerable position, it would seem to him that she'd have moved back to Atlanta to be closer to the action. But then, maybe she was just more subtle than the usual run of opportunists.

The devil take La Dooley! Alice had offered him a place to recuperate, and unless the big blonde went into action and called a press conference right here on the island—about as likely as Stone's winning a Pulitzer prize for the series he'd done on archaeological piracy—he was damned well going to do just that. Recuperate.

With that end in mind, he had selected a book from the cottage's shelves of dog-eared paperbacks and read until he'd fallen asleep on the sofa last night. He'd wakened just before dawn, at which time he had gone to bed to sleep another few hours.

Quiet. It was a luxury he could easily become addicted to.

He'd checked her cottage first thing upon awakening and seen no sign of life. But then, La Dooley was probably the type who played all night and slept until the sun was well over the yardarm. Which meant the mornings, at least, would belong to him.

At nine he had made himself a sandwich and a pot of coffee for breakfast. At 9:37, feeling remarkably fit considering the bloody and broken mess he'd been when they had hauled his carcass out of Africa a few months ago, he strolled down to the water and launched himself on the inner tube.

Approximately half an hour later, Stone got his first good look at the woman he'd been sent down to Coronoke Island to keep under surveillance.

He'd expected her to be attractive. His aunt had prepared him for that. Billy's taste in women usually ran to showy types, which was why Stone hadn't expected a little oatmeal-faced debutante.

But La Dooley wasn't a little anything. What she was, was . . . well, *big*. Big frame, narrow waist, full breasts, generous hips. Legs that started at ground level and steepled all the way up to the stratosphere. Las Vegas showgirl big. Triple-dip, sugar-cone big.

A mullet jumped not three feet away and Stone ignored it, still staring at the big blonde who had taken his little cousin for over half a million and was threatening to come back for seconds. It wasn't going to take a pair of binoculars and any cloak-and-dagger activity to keep up with La Dooley. If there was one thing she was, it was visible!

Her hairstyle, if you could call it a style, was kinky, streaky and blond, looking as if it hadn't seen a comb in six months. From this distance, it looked almost natural, but then, on what she'd gouged out of Billy, she could afford the best salon treatment. If what Alice Hardisson had told him was even partially true, she could afford to fly to Paris once a week to have her legs waxed!

Evidently, she'd figured on a bit of privacy to recharge her batteries and work on her story. She wasn't
dressed for an audience. Instead, she was wearing baggy
sweats, a pair of shades and, unless he was mistaken, that
was an apple she had clutched in her teeth. The symbol-
ism of it suddenly struck him and he began to chuckle.
Still grinning at his small private joke, he began paddling toward the shore. The layer of pink on his shoulders, thighs and belly that he'd collected the day before
had soaked in overnight, but Stone didn't kid himself that
he was in any condition to stay out through the middle of
the day, sunscreen or no sunscreen. From his mother,
who'd been Alice Hardisson's sister, he'd inherited his
height and his dark hair. The paternal side of his heri-
tage was pure Highland Scot. Gray eyes, stainless-steel
backbone, a taste for Celtic music and a hide that, without some preliminary weathering, tended to burn.

He had lost his weathering, along with a few quarts of
blood and more than a few pounds, but he was working
on it.

Besides, it wouldn't hurt to take a closer look at his
quarry. As distasteful as he found the whole business, he
had given Alice his word that he'd keep the woman away
from the gutter press. Alice had done her part by isolat-
ing La Dooley in a place with no phones, no fax, limited
mail service and no reporters. The rest was up to him.

The trouble was, he hadn't even started yet and already he was beginning to feel a little bit foolish. He was
a journalist. He'd done his share of investigative journalism, but something about this assignment stuck in his
craw.

By the time Stone reached shore, La Dooley had disappeared. He figured she'd probably wanted to scope out
the territory—maybe drop in on the Keegans and check

on the radio link to the outside world. If she was smart—
and most predators were—she'd be wanting to get her
bearings before she made her move.

If she made her move. Even steel magnolias like Alice
Hardisson had been known to make a mistake.

Reluctantly, Lucy turned to go back inside. In spite of
her dark glasses, the sun was blinding. She'd forgotten
just how bright it could be near the water, even with the
sky beginning to haze over. At the door to her cottage,
she yawned, stretched and marveled all over again that
she was actually here instead of back in her own swelter-
ing apartment poring over the help wanteds and listening with one ear for the commode to stop running. It
took three jiggles after each flush, and she did it so au-
tomatically that she couldn't always remember whether
or not she'd forgotten.

She made a pitcher of iced tea and carried it out onto
the screened deck. That and the apple she had consumed
earlier constituted breakfast. Maybe tomorrow she would
fry up a can of corned-beef hash with onions and catsup
for breakfast. That had been Pawpaw's favorite. Familiar foods and familiar music always gave her a safe,
comfortable feeling. Maybe she would write to Lillian
and Ollie Mae, for old times' sake.

Or maybe she'd simply vegetate. This was a vacation.
Vacations were for being lazy and indulging whims. No
telling when she'd get another one.

The trouble was, she was just too excited to vegetate.
After showering, she unpacked a pair of shorts and a
T-shirt and set off to explore her new surroundings, lux-
uriating in the raw-silk feel of pine straw under her bare
feet and the total absence of traffic noises.

The only sign of life at any of the other cottages was a lineful of towels and bathing suits. Earlier, she'd heard the sound of an outboard heading over to Hatteras. So be it. She liked privacy.

And really, she wasn't lonely. There were plenty of other people around if she got tired of her own company. The Keegans, for instance. And the reclusive bird-watcher, who was supposed to be her closest neighbor.

All the same, by early afternoon, having walked around the entire island, pausing to watch birds, distant fishermen, even more distant windsurfers, and to examine a set of footprints in the sand—long, fairly narrow, naked and probably male—she was beginning to feel a bit like Robinson Crusoe.

Her stomach growled. She breathed deeply of the fragrance of sun-warmed cedars and salt marsh as she reluctantly turned back toward Heron's Rest. Funny— when she had accepted this windfall vacation from her ex-mother-in-law, after the first few minutes of shock, all she'd been able to think about was having an entire summer with no clock to punch and no one to fuss at her for playing her music too loud at night. As guilty as she'd felt for accepting anything at all from a Hardisson, she hadn't been able to resist the lure of a few lazy, idyllic weeks all to herself. But already she was getting restless.

Not only that, she felt guilty. She despised Billy Hardisson, partly because he was a despicable person, but mostly because, with his courtly manners and his easy-going charm, he had made her feel like a lady. And it had all been a lie.

Alice was a lady. Billy was Nothing dressed up like Something. But for a little while he had made her feel special, made her feel beautiful, made her feel wanted as a person and not just for her body.

Of course, he'd wanted that, too, but when she'd refused to go to bed with him, he hadn't called her names. Instead, he'd turned up the charm another notch.

The creep. The only decent thing about Billy Hardisson was his mother, and Lucy felt sorry for the poor woman. According to Lucy's father, a lady was a woman who served his beer in a glass. Lucy had learned from Alice Hardisson that there was a bit more to being a lady than that, which was why she had quietly left town three years ago without telling anyone how she had come to lose her baby. The only other person in the house the day it had happened had been the maid, but she wouldn't talk. She was Liam and Mellie's niece. She owed her allegiance to the Hardissons.

Someday poor Alice was going to have her heart broken, but at least Lucy wouldn't be a part of it.

Yawning, she shucked off unpleasant thoughts of the past. Last night she had read an entire paperback romance, and she intended to read another one tonight. But with the sun shining, the birds singing and all those endless acres of saltwater beckoning, she wasn't about to spend the daylight hours reading, too.

"Time for a new adventure, li'l sugar." She could hear Pawpaw now. That ol' highway wasn't a-rollin' out before her, but all that water surely was. So why not take out one of the boats tied up at the pier for the use of the renters? It had been years since she had handled a boat. If she was going to make a fool of herself, she'd just as soon do it without an audience.

Lucy made herself a peanut butter sandwich and ate it as she sauntered down to the pier, where a tall, rugged-looking man with a distinctly military bearing greeted her from the stern of a red inboard.

He introduced himself as Maudie Keegan's husband, Rich, and told her he was on his way over to Hatteras. "But if you need me to check you out on a boat, that's what I'm here for." As good as his word, he took time to show her the basics after clamping an outboard motor on the stern of one of the smaller boats.

Dressed in a pair of paint-stained khakis and little else, Rich Keegan exuded a potent brand of masculinity. Lucy's instinctive wariness rose up defensively, but so far as she could see, there wasn't even a hint of speculation in his bright blue eyes as he handed her down into the aluminum skiff. She wished she'd kept on her sweats, but in the heat of the day, they were just too hot. Her shorts and camp shirt were old, loose and deliberately designed to disguise her natural attributes. Even Alice would have approved of their faded modesty. Besides, she wasn't in purdah. Not even Alice and her blue-haired, old-monied friends would expect her to suffocate.

Forgetting her self-consciousness, Lucy concentrated on Keegan's instructions. He made her go through the routine until he was satisfied she had it down pat, and then he pointed out the channel markers. "Hang to the left of the red ones if you're headed over to Hatteras, to the right on the way back out. Watch out for shoals. The tide's about slack now, but it'll turn within the half hour. Don't go out of sight of land in case the weather closes in. And, Ms. Dooley, I understand you're a certified life-guard, but do me a favor? Wear this thing, anyway." He reached past her, and Lucy stepped back suddenly. The boat lurched, and she would have gone over the side if he hadn't grabbed her.

"Whoops! Sorry," she said breathlessly when he released her shoulders and handed her an orange life vest. "No sea legs."

"You'll get the hang of it. These aluminum boats are durable, but they're a little like a canoe until you get used to them. Fortunately, the water's shallow around these parts—you can't get in a whole lot of trouble if you use some common sense. But we have these rules, so wear the thing for me, will you?"

"Scout's honor." When Lucy grinned, Rich grinned back, and she was suddenly glad he was spoken for. With a man like Rich Keegan, she just might be tempted to forget how rotten her judgment was where men were concerned.

Rich had his rules, and well, Lucy had hers, too. And survival rule number one was to avoid anything that even *looked* like temptation.

After waving him off, she repeated his instructions—or rather, her interpretation of his instructions—until she was certain she had it grooved into her brain. It was pretty much like her father's instructions for starting the old Dooley Trolley. She had learned to drive that when she was twelve.

"Pull the whoosie halfway out, set the whatsit, push the do-jigger, shove the whoosie back a third and pray." Wrinkling her nose in concentration, she mumbled the incantation, went through the motions, and miraculously—it worked!

Pulling away from the pier at a sedate three knots, Lucy wished her sixth-graders could see her now. They teased her unmercifully about the clunker she drove. She teased right back by telling them that it took far more skill to drive a *real* car than it did to operate any one of the sleek new computerized models that were designed by robots for robots.

By the time she had circled the island twice, Lucy was high on the sheer exhilaration of accomplishment. Taking dead aim at a channel marker, she was following the deep green water, steering close to a high shoal that ran along the southwest tip of Hatteras Island, when it occurred to her the sun was no longer blazing down on the back of her neck.

Blazing? It was no longer even visible! While she'd been busy learning to navigate, a thick bank of black clouds had snuck up and swallowed every visible scrap of blue.

Uneasily, Lucy peered at the sky again. She'd been skirting the landward edge of the channel, marveling at the way the water magnified the size of the few shells hugging the side of the steep shoal. Scallop shells looked like dinner plates. That oyster shell was easily a foot long, and—

And then she saw the conch shell. Only a few yards ahead, it was as big as a basketball. She reminded herself that it was only an illusion, but all the same, it was tempting. Half a minute more and she could snare it for her class. They might even make a study of the magnifying powers of water.

Having rationalized the collecting of her souvenir, Lucy adjusted the throttle and idled closer, careful to stay just over into the deep water. The moment she came within reach, she grabbed an oar with one hand, meaning to work the tip of the blade into the opening of the shell and lift it aboard. Carefully balancing, she leaned over the side of the unsteady craft.

Lightning flashed. A split second later there was a blast of thunder. Jerking around to glance over her shoulder, Lucy gasped at the angry mass roiling directly overhead. Cold sweat broke out on her back and she swore under her breath. A single moment's inattention was all it took. Before she could gather her wits, several things happened at once. The blade of the oar dipped under the water, causing the boat to swerve into the shoal. Before she could shove off again, the outboard sputtered and died.

"Oh, no!" Lucy lunged for the choke, then grabbed the throttle. Too late. "Oh, damn and blast!" she wailed as another burst of lightning split the tarnished sky.

A splash of rain struck the back of her neck and channeled down under her damp shirt. Sweat prickled under the life vest. "All right now, Lucinda, calm down," she muttered. "First push the— No, pull the whoosie halfway out, then push the whatsit and— Oh, *rats!*"

On the raw edge of panic, she worked the throttle several times, stabbing the starter button in between. Nothing happened.

Lightning flashed again. The thunder was almost constant now. A bloom of iridescence spread swiftly around the stern of the boat, and Lucy stared at it in resignation.

She had flooded the blasted motor. Which meant she would have to wait for it to cool off before she could even try it again. Which meant she was going to get soaked, at the very least. Possibly fried.

Lightning flickered green against a black sky. Cats' paws ruffled the dark surface of the water, and she buried her face in her crossed arms and swore softly. Was it just her, or was it something in the Dooley family gene pool that inhibited the development of ordinary common sense?

She should've suspected something was wrong when, after growing up like a gypsy, she'd been so eager for a real home and a real family that she'd nearly run off and married a charming rat whose idea of fidelity was never sleeping with more than one woman at the same time.

That had been in Baton Rouge. She'd been seventeen when she had fallen in love with Hamm Sheppard's family, which had consisted of parents, a grandmother and seven brothers and sisters, all of whom had lived in the same house for three generations.

Fortunately, Pawpaw had loaded up the Dooley Trolley and lit out for Galveston before she could get into too much trouble.

That had been her first near miss, but certainly not her last. How many times had she mistaken lust for something more lasting, more meaningful? Not that she'd ever been promiscuous, but even that had been due more to an innate sense of self-respect than any sense of self-preservation.

When it came to brains, Lucy thought as she attempted to row herself back to Coronoke and safety, hers were about as reliable as a two-dollar watch. At this rate, she might as well just grab a live wire and be done with it.

Stone had been watching through the binoculars when his neighbor sauntered down the path toward the pier earlier that day, minus the sweats. The woman had legs, all right. The kind of legs a man woke up in the middle of the night dreaming about. Long, golden, silky confections with flawlessly turned ankles and calves designed expressly to fit a man's palms.

And then there were her thighs....

Slowly, he lowered the binoculars and exhaled in a soft whistle. So that was La Dooley. In the flesh! If the rest of her lived up to those legs at closer inspection, he could easily see how Billy might have lost his perspective. No wonder she'd been able to twist him and a whole damned law firm around her little finger. If Alice hadn't been off on one of her constant jaunts, it never would have happened. But when the cat was away, all hell usually broke loose.

Stone just hoped she'd been worth it, especially since she was reportedly trying to elbow her way back up to the trough. His worn mocs silent on the sandy, leaf-strewn path, he followed her down to the pier in time to watch her give Keegan the business.

She was good, all right—he had to hand it to her. First the smile. Roughly a thousand watts, he figured. Easily enough to stun a full-grown ox. Somewhere along the line, she had cultivated this way of standing with her toes turned in like a barefoot kid, and scratching her thigh in a way that was obviously designed to call attention to her assets. In a centerfold type like La Dooley, the effect was lethal.

Billy, poor devil, had never stood a chance.

Stone watched as she pretended to trip, forcing Keegan to catch her by the shoulders. A pretty shopworn ploy, but Keegan didn't seem to mind.

Having known a few women who made a profession of preying on men, Stone felt anger begin to curdle inside him. He'd been too smart to fall into that particular trap, but more than one of his friends had been ripped up pretty badly by women like Lucy Dooley.

As for Stone, he'd once had a shot at a good relationship a long time ago. He'd blown it all by himself, but that didn't mean he was going to stand by and let La Dooley mess up another life. Keegan and Maudie seemed to be pretty decent people. The first time the ex-Mrs. Hardisson tried anything there, Stone was going to take her aside and quietly drive home a few basic rules.

In fact, he was beginning to look forward to it.

Keegan's runabout pulled away first, heading east toward Hatteras. La Dooley went next and took a different direction. Stone felt some of the tension bleed away. Then, having nothing better to do with his time, he collected his field guide to Eastern birds from the cottage and, binoculars around his neck, made himself comfortable in the shade of a sprawling live oak.

She circled the island a few times. He followed her by sound. A pelican—a brown pelican, to be more specific—flapped by, lumbering along like a C-130 cargo plane. He followed it out of sight and then picked up La Dooley as she rounded a wooded point on the southwest side of the island. From there she cut a figure eight and then headed toward Hatteras Inlet.

The sun was gone, taking the edge off the heat, but the humidity still hovered in the high nineties. Leaving his book and his glasses behind, Stone loped back up the path and returned a few minutes later with a cold beer and a slab of cheese. A little ways out from shore, a flock of black, white and orange birds were hammering on something just under the surface of the water. Dutifully, he identified them as oyster catchers. At this rate, he could qualify for a whole new area of reporting. In which case he might be bored out of his gourd, but he probably wouldn't get blown up with any great regularity.

He watched a flock of crows worry the hell out of a sea gull, noticing as he did that the storm was almost overhead. By the time the first jagged streak of lightning sliced across the sky, he was already racing toward the pier. In the preternatural darkness, he could barely make out the low profile of an aluminum boat with a single passenger. It was about a mile out, and the boat wasn't moving.

Was she *crazy?* Did she have some kind of a death wish? Leaving her to her fate might solve a few of the Hardisson's more pressing problems, but Stone didn't think his aunt Alice would want that on her conscience.

By the time the second blister had formed and burst on her palm, Lucy was chilled to the bone. She couldn't remember the last time she had rowed a boat, but she did know it had been a wooden one, not one of these blasted tippy aluminum jobs!

Wasn't metal an excellent conductor of electricity? Oh, God....

Lightning was almost continuous now, the rain blowing in soft, horizontal sheets. It wasn't really cold, yet she couldn't seem to stop shivering. Whoever had designed these blasted life vests ought to have to dance naked in one of the things! She wasn't in danger of drowning, dammit, she was in danger of being chafed to death! If she didn't get blown out of the water first.

"Thirty-four—unh!—years old, and—unh!—don't even have the brains to—unh!—come in out of the—" Clamping one oar between elbow and knee, she shoved her hair out of her eyes. Rain, salt air and naturally curly hair were a disastrous combination. She'd been trying to let her hair grow out so she could braid it, pin it up and thereby achieve some degree of neatness, but the first thing she was going to do when she got in—*if* she got in— was shave her head!

With rain pounding the surface of the water, drumming on the battered metal boat, Lucy didn't even hear the outboard until it was right on top of her.

"Hi, there! Ahoy!"

Shoving the tangle of sodden hair from her eyes once more, she looked up to see the man just as he grabbed hold of her boat. "You're speaking to me?" The look he gave her didn't bear analysis, but it was not lust she saw in those chilly gray eyes. "Sorry. I didn't hear you drive up."

"You didn't hear me drive up. Right," Stone repeated, unsure whether she was mocking him or he was mocking her. "Unless you've got a death wish, ship your oars, tilt your motor and throw me your towline."

In the end, Stone boarded her skiff and carried out his own commands. It seemed to be the only way to get them moving. The woman was either brain dead or paralyzed. Her legs were covered with goose bumps, and even that, he noted with disgust, didn't lessen their impact. His fingers were itching to tangle themselves in that mop of kinky, streaky hair and jerk some sense into her devious little brain, but he was distracted by a streak of lightning, followed almost immediately by a blast of thunder.

"Get into my boat," he snapped. "Yours'll tow faster light. Come on, lady, just move it, will you? I'm in no mood to risk my neck just to save yours!"

And despite his surliness, Lucy was in no mood to argue. As stiff as she was from rowing and shivering, one glance at the stern, dripping wet face looming over her was enough to force her reluctant muscles to cooperate.

Stone didn't waste time. While she huddled on the center thwart, hugging her wet, goose-bumpy knees with equally wet, goose-bumpy arms, he piloted them toward shore. The worst of the storm had already passed overhead and was headed for the northern villages on Hatteras Island.

The rain continued to fall.

And Lucy continued to shiver.

Neither of them spoke. Even if he'd been inclined to yell over all the noise, Stone didn't think she wanted to hear anything he might have to say at the moment.

Besides, he had come to the island for a purpose. Driving her away wasn't going to do the job. If she left, he'd feel obligated to follow her, and he wasn't ready to quit this place yet.

With swift efficiency, he secured both boats and then reached out to help her up onto the pier. Lucy couldn't repress a gasp when his hard, salty palm grasped hers.

He narrowed those icy gray eyes at her. "You got a problem?"

Lucy shook her head. She had a problem—she had a lot of problems, but she didn't think he really wanted to hear them. "No, b-b-but thanks for rescuing me. I th-think I must have fl-flooded the c-c-carburator."

Stone's wide, mobile mouth turned down at the corners. He didn't want her thanks. He didn't want anything to do with her. He sure as hell didn't want to start feeling sorry for her just because she was wet and cold and maybe a little bit scared—if she had sense enough to be scared. If she had sense enough even to know what might have happened to her out there.

At the moment she looked more like a big-eyed, waterlogged, oversize waif than a man-eating witch with a cash register for a heart. In spite of what he knew about her, Stone felt a growing urge to gather her into his arms and hold her there until her teeth stopped chattering.

He told himself that the concussion he'd suffered back in March must have shaken loose a few too many gray cells. "Better get out of those wet things," he muttered. "Go have a hot soak and a stiff drink—make you feel better."

She nodded jerkily. Her eyes were nearly on a level with his. Stone liked his women petite, feminine and easy to get along with, and this one was none of the above. Her hair was all over her face again. She was a real mess, but somehow, that didn't seem to diminish that sultry appeal of hers. It was screwy.

"Go!" he barked, and she turned and plodded up the pier, bare feet splashing unheedingly through the puddles.

And that was another thing, dammit. Her feet. They weren't what he'd expected, and that made him angry. Women's feet were supposed to be pampered and shapely, with painted toenails. Hers were short, broad and squared-off at the toes. The kind of feet he'd seen in too many parts of the world where kids grew up without shoes, sometimes without parents and, all too often, without food.

Swearing, he collected his sodden field guide and the binoculars, which he'd had the foresight to put back into the case, and started up the path, wishing he had headed north to this old fishing shack he knew about in Maine instead of letting Alice talk him into doing her scut work for her.

"Ahhh—*choo!*"

"Jeez, lady! Give me a break, will you?"

Lucy blinked her red-rimmed eyes at the lanky figure leaning up against her dogwood tree. She had awakened with a scratchy throat, itchy eyes and a chestful of cinder blocks. "That's my tree. Go lean on your own tree," she grumbled, not even feeling guilty about it. He had rescued her yesterday, and she had thanked him. As far as she was concerned, they were even.

She sneezed again, and Stone shoved himself away from the tree trunk where he had been watching some kind of big bird carrying sticks to build a nest. "You scared my hawk," he accused.

"Excuse me, but if it's in my tree, then it's *my* hawk. Go find your own hawk."

"You look like the devil."

She sent him a resentful look. "I don't doubt you're in a position to know firsthand."

He glowered some more. The trouble was, she *didn't* look like the devil. Even with her hair uncombed, her eyes and nose red and a bathrobe that would have shamed a professional beggar, she looked . . .

Sexy. About a thousand volts of sheer, uninsulated sexuality.

"Ahhh-choo!"

"Go to bed," he muttered.

"Go to hell," she muttered back.

"Go with me," he retorted, eyeing the front of her soft cotton wrap. If she was wearing anything under it, it didn't show. He could see the shape of her breasts and the placement of her nipples, and when his loins tightened in response, he swore again.

To bed or to hell? Lucy wanted to ask, but for once, common sense came to her rescue. Without another word, she turned and stalked back inside her cottage.

Dammit, she had wanted to go lie on the beach and let the sun bake the aches from her body. Now, thanks to her nosy, nasty-tempered, bird-gawking neighbor, she couldn't even do that!

And that was another thing—weren't bird-watchers supposed to be mild-mannered types who minded their own business? Middle-aged men in knee socks, baggy shorts and pith helmets?

Whoever heard of a bird-watcher in faded, skin-tight jeans—one with ice gray eyes in a lean, sexy face?

Lucy knew about men. She'd been fighting them off since puberty, with varying degrees of success. Lillian had said it was the way she looked, but she didn't look any different from thousands of other women, only taller than most. Her blond hair was sun streaked because of all the time she spent lifeguarding. It was naturally curly, which meant that if she wanted to control it at all, she either had to cut it two inches short or let it grow out, and no matter how many times she'd tried, she'd never had the patience to let it grow much beyond its current unmanageable length.

The fact that she had dark brown lashes and brows to match her eyes was a help, because she was allergic to cosmetics, even a few of the hypoallergenic ones. She couldn't wear sunscreen, much less perfume, but fortunately she had the kind of skin that tanned on the first day of spring and stayed that way through Labor Day.

Nor had she ever deliberately dressed to get attention. The plain truth was, her taste in clothes had been pretty awful until a few years ago. It had been Alice who'd shown her how to downplay her flamboyant looks by wearing muted colors and conservative styles.

She'd been wearing her old blue tank bathing suit when Billy had first seen her at the club pool working with a group of floaters. From then on, he had haunted the pool, watching her give lessons, bringing her drinks, slathering lotion on her back, which she'd had to shower off immediately and then explain about the itchy rashes— and then allow him to buy her lunch to make up for making him feel guilty.

He'd been fun, and he was certainly good-looking. Naturally, she'd been flattered. When he'd learned she was attending night school, he'd started following her to class and waiting for her to come out. He had bought her flowers and candy and a gold watch with five diamonds on each side, which she'd refused because Lillian had told her that while jewelry was real nice, a lady didn't accept expensive jewelry from a man unless she was willing to go to bed with him.

So she had given back the watch and tried to explain why she couldn't sleep with him, which was how he'd discovered her secret weakness.

All she really wanted was a home and a family. Nothing fancy, just a small house with a yard big enough for a garden patch, and after a while, a few babies.

And so he'd offered her the one thing she couldn't refuse, and she hadn't refused. They had married in South Carolina and honeymooned in St. Thomas, and Lucy had thought for a little while her dreams had come true. Of course, the house Billy had surprised her with had been designed more for show than for comfort. She'd never felt truly at home there, but she hadn't wanted to hurt his feelings. As for the yard, most of it had been taken up with a swimming pool and a few square yards of green-velvet grass, but she'd had hopes of turning the grass into a vegetable patch. Oh, she'd been full of hopes....

Men! She sneezed five times in a row on her way to the kitchen to make herself a mug of hot tea, and wished she had a cinnamon stick to stir it with. When she was a little girl, Ollie Mae had dosed her summer colds with cinnamon tea. It had always seemed to help.

Or maybe just having someone care enough to fuss over her had made it seem that way.

Stone waited for more than an hour to see if she'd show. When she didn't, he felt reprieved. Whatever her plans were, she wasn't going to be making any sudden moves for the next day or so. She looked like hell and sounded worse.

Correction. She *should've* looked like hell. Unfortunately, the image that lingered in his mind was of a pair of legs he'd like to take a year off to explore, a tantalizing hint of hidden treasures just waiting to be discovered and a pair of wide, full lips and sleepy-lidded eyes that spelled *sex* in any language in the world.

Not for the first time, Stone wondered if he'd made a major mistake by accepting his aunt's offer of a quiet place to recuperate in exchange for a small favor.

Three

———

For two days Lucy slept. In her bed, on her screened deck and on the white-sand beach. She ate sparingly, partly because she could never remember whether she should starve a cold and feed a fever or vice versa, but mostly because she didn't feel like fixing meals.

On the third day, she sprawled in the cedar deck lounge, a cooling bowl of canned vegetable soup on the table beside her, and strummed random chords on her guitar, which was badly out of tune.

So was she. Colds always made her feel grungy. This time she had the added displeasure of seeing her foul-tempered neighbor lurking in the woods with his binoculars and his blasted bird book every time she looked outside.

Didn't he have any birds on his side of the island? Did he have to hunt hers?

The fact that his side of the island also happened to be her side, as the cottages stood not five hundred feet apart, didn't excuse the fact that every time she opened her eyes, he was somewhere about, with his floppy black hair and his faded jeans, his frigid gray eyes—which she couldn't see from there—and his sensuously chiseled mouth, which she could.

Birders. A more useless lot she had yet to see!

On the fourth day, she felt almost human again. She stood under the shower, letting the smelly, lukewarm groundwater stream over her head and shoulders, until the quietly humming generator reminded her that resources on Coronoke were not to be squandered.

Two peanut butter sandwiches later, she ventured out, having first ascertained that her nosy neighbor was nowhere in sight. Five minutes later she rapped on the frame of the Keegans' screen door. "Hi! Anyone home?"

Maudie appeared, a paintbrush in one hand and a dirty rag in the other. "Stone said you had a cold. I was going to come over today with chicken soup, but I got to painting and lost track of time."

"I opened a can."

"My homemade's better. You're feeling better, then?"

"Much. Sleep usually does it for me." She fingered a tube of acrylic paint. "Stone. Is he the bird-watcher? I suppose he told you he had to tow me in the other day when I flooded my outboard—your outboard, that is—in the middle of a thunderstorm."

"Rich saw you two headed in. He said you got soaked. One thing about the weather here, it's seldom boring."

Maudie insisted on pouring them tall glasses of ice tea, which they took out to the garden, where she showed off her vegetables. "Root crops do great as long as you add lots of compost. And as long as the tide doesn't come up too high. Wait'll you taste my sweet onions."

They talked vegetables for a while, and Lucy told her something about the only garden she'd ever had, belonging to one of her father's many mistresses—which led to still another discussion.

By the time they wandered back into the house, Lucy felt as if she had found a friend. She nearly fell apart when Maudie confided that she was four months pregnant, but that was probably only the aftermath of her cold. Colds always left her feeling weepy.

"I'm hoping for a boy," the small, tanned woman confided. "I already have a daughter, and she'll be having her first about the same time I'm having this one."

Lucy's eyes widened, and Maudie laughed. "I'll be forty when this one's born. Rich feeds me vitamins and tries to make me take a nap every day. Lord knows how he'll be as a father. Probably spoil the poor little lump to death. I wish you could've seen him when he found out. For a minute I thought he was going to swoon. Turned white as a sheet, but then he raised his fist in the air, jumped three feet off the ground and shouted, '*Yeah!*'" She grinned, her nice green eyes crinkling with warm laughter. "Threw his back out doing it, too. I had to baby him for a solid week, but he's worth it."

It had to be the remnants of her cold, Lucy thought a few minutes later as she made her way back to the cottage. Red nose, eyes tearing up at the thought of that tall, military type and his sweet, pregnant little Maudie. She felt warm and weepy and more than a little bit envious. Sniffling, she wiped an arm over her drenched eyes and walked head-on into the man who stepped out from behind a tree.

"Whoa!" he said.

"Oh, for heaven's sake, can't you watch where you're going?" She stepped back and crossed her arms over her chest. "Don't you have anything better to do than jump out from behind trees and scare the wits out of people?"

"Well, now that you mention it, I do occasionally rescue brain-dead bimbos who lack the common sense to stay in out of the rain."

"If you mean me, it wasn't raining when I set out. There wasn't a cloud in the sky."

"No thunderbolts, either, right?"

"Give me credit for—" She broke off, shaking her head. "Why do I bother even trying to justify myself?"

"I don't know. Why do you?" Stone mused. He hadn't just imagined it. Close up, she was unbelievable. No natural blonde could have brows and lashes that dark. Her mouth had that swollen, bee-stung look that women seemed to go for these day. In her case, it was probably silicon. If the stuff ever started sliding, that stubborn little chin of hers might not look quite so tempting. Or quite so challenging.

They were doing a measured dance on the narrow path, simultaneously stepping first to the left and then to the right. Exasperated, Stone grabbed a handful of faded pink T-shirt and thrust her to one side. Then he dropped his hand, bowed and watched her stalk off, those elegant legs of hers flashing in the sun like a pair of precision-turned bronze pistons.

God, what a woman. Even knowing what she was, he was so steamed up it was going to take a long, cold shower—or a five-mile swim—to bring him back down.

When it dawned on him belatedly that she'd been crying, he frowned. And then he shrugged. Probably picked up her mail and found a note from her banker—low tide in the old checking account.

For the next two days, Lucy was determined to avoid Stone, and Stone was equally determined to avoid Lucy. Both succeeded. Stone forced himself to relax. He watched birds, and even got so he could identify a few species without reference to his guide. At night he read. Early mornings, when he was pretty sure La Dooley would still be sleeping, he swam, concentrating on his breaststroke in an effort to rebuild muscles that had been torn by the explosion.

Swimming made him hungry, and he discovered a heretofore unsuspected talent for concocting fanciful sandwiches. Once he'd perfected his sardine, Swiss cheese and sauerkraut creation, he turned his talents to redefining the Italian sub. Which meant that sooner or later he would need to locate the nearest deli and lay in a fresh supply of ingredients.

Lucy prowled. A creature of habit, she hardly knew what to do with all the empty hours in the day. Accustomed to rising at six to do her housework and laundry before school, teaching a full day and then coming home to class prep, grading papers and a weekend job at the steak house, she had trouble adjusting her internal speedometer, which was set on Rush and Hurry.

She would have preferred to swim before breakfast, but that was when her nosy neighbor chose to swim, in the only water deep enough for decent swimming without wading a mile offshore. So she puttered about in the shallows off her own cottage, knowing he was probably watching her through those blasted binoculars of his!

Which was paranoid, she'd be the first to admit. He was watching birds, and birds were everywhere, and it was a free country.

All the same, she couldn't seem to stop thinking about him, and that bothered her. He wasn't what you'd call handsome. Not the way Billy had been handsome, with his perfect teeth and his perfect features and his perfect salon tan and his blow-dried hair.

This man was a slob. Either he had a wardrobe of identically disreputable jeans and limp khaki shirts or he'd worn the same clothes every day since she'd been here. He usually needed a shave, he had a diabolical smile and his manners would have disgraced Attila the Hun.

Without coming within a hundred feet of her, he made her edgy. Dammit, he was spoiling her vacation, just by being on the same island.

Lucy fretted. She was nibbling too much when she shouldn't, not eating enough when she should and hardly sleeping at all. The neat oval fingernails she had been so proud of began to disappear. She *never* chewed her nails unless she was truly frazzled. The last time they'd been this short had been . . . about three years ago?

Precisely three years ago.

She practiced on her guitar, singing in the husky, off-key alto that no amount of glee club and choir practice had ever managed to improve. Finally, determined to lay her ghosts, she changed into her tank suit, snatched up her sunglasses and stalked across the island to where the water was chest deep and clear of obstacles. There, without once looking over her shoulder to see if her nemesis was lurking behind a tree with his binoculars focused on her, she swam laps between a set of homemade channel markers until she was utterly winded, and then she slogged ashore, spoiling for a fight.

Unfortunately—or perhaps fortunately—she didn't meet a soul on her way back to the cottage.

The next day she followed the same routine and then flopped on the beach for a nap. Her perennial light tan had already deepened to bronze, and she told herself she would pay for it in years to come, but she could hardly swim in sweats and a straw hat, and she refused to wait until after the sun went down!

Pleasantly drowsy after her morning workout and a lunch of two boiled eggs, a diet cola and a candy bar, Lucy was dozing on the deck over a biography she'd been meaning to read for years when Stone McCloud appeared at her door.

"I'm headed across to Hatteras for supplies. Do you need anything?"

She sat up and rubbed her eyes. The book, a candy wrapper and her drugstore reading glasses slid to the floor as she blinked through the screen. "Supplies?"

"Food. Mail. Whatever."

"Oh. You're taking one of the boats?" It was hot and humid, and her brain was still half-asleep.

"No, lady, I'm walking on water."

"Are you allowed to leave here?"

"What do you mean *allowed?*" he asked suspiciously.

Lucy yawned. Rising in one fluid motion, she crossed to the door and peered through the screen at the lean, rangy figure standing on the doorstep, hands rammed into his hip pockets. "I thought maybe you'd been exiled here—you know, like the Birdman of Alcatraz? But I guess even he had to eat."

Without a word, Stone turned and left, and Lucy watched him head toward the pier. Acting purely on impulse, she retrieved her purse from inside the cottage and followed a few minutes later.

He was no more than a dozen yards out when she untied the second skiff and cranked the outboard. At the sound, he glanced over his shoulder and scowled, and Lucy smiled sweetly. They continued at that pace, a dozen yards apart, all the way to the marina on the lower end of Hatteras. Stone had already secured his boat and was watching her like a hawk when she eased up alongside the wharf. He held out a hand, and she tossed him her painter, wishing she could strangle him with it. She didn't like him, didn't trust him—didn't trust any man. The fact that he obviously felt the same way about her, for no reason at all, was beginning to grate on her nerves.

His car was one of those macho models that probably cost more than she made in a year. Naturally. And naturally, it had to be parked right next to her old beige clunker in the row of spaces assigned to the tenants of Coronoke's five cottages.

Neither of them spoke until Stone unlocked his car and opened the door. He deliberately waited until she'd dug her keys out of her purse and then taunted, "Need a ride?"

"No, thanks." Lucy smiled sweetly, hoping his car wouldn't start.

Shrugging, he lowered himself into the driver's seat. It occurred to her that for someone who looked so fit, he moved rather stiffly. Almost as if he were afraid moving would hurt.

Stone pulled up at the deli, and Lucy pulled in beside him. Side by side, they mounted the wide wooden steps. Stone bought several types of cheese, a variety of cold cuts and two six-packs of Mexican beer. Lucy bought cold fried chicken, macaroni and cheese, five chocolate bars and two six-packs of diet cola.

From there they both drove to the closest supermarket, where each took a cart and headed in opposite directions.

Lucy left first, carrying two sacks of canned goods and cookies and wearing a new straw hat—neon pink with an orange-and-lime-green band decorated with a glittery blue plastic swordfish. It suited her mood to perfection.

From there she went to the real estate office to pick up her mail and place a call to Frank. She'd forgotten to tell him the feeding schedule for her African violets.

She had just started digging out change when Stone pulled in next to the two pay phones. "Nice hat," he said with a nasty grin.

At least, she told herself it was a nasty grin. The truth was, it was a rather attractive grin, chipped front tooth and all, if one could ignore those cool gray eyes.

"You can borrow my charge card if you don't have enough change. Important call?"

"No, thank you, and yes—it's an important call. Don't let me keep you." She began laying out quarters and dimes on the shelf below the phone.

Stone leaned over and spoke softly against her right ear, sending a rush of chill bumps down her side. "If you won't use my card, at least let me lend you some change."

Lucy jumped and brushed her hand over her right cheek, which was still tingling from the contact. "I don't want your card, I don't want your money. There's only one thing I want from you, Mr. McCloud—your absence. *Leave me alone!*"

"The name is Stone."

"How fitting," she jeered. Jeering didn't come naturally to Lucy, but she was learning.

He lifted his eyebrows. This time his grin was unmistakably suggestive. "You noticed."

Lucy ignored the double entendre. Were all men this way with all women? Crude to the point of being deliberately offensive. Or was it only with her? Had Lillian

been right all those years ago when she had warned a
troubled girl hovering on the brink of adolescence that
boys would always take one look at her and think of only
one thing?

"Lucy? What is it? Are you all right?"

Lips clamped tightly against a tendency to tremble, she
met his eyes—hers large and dark with hurt, his cool,
wary and increasingly puzzled. "Lucy?" he repeated, and
she lifted her head and deliberately turned her back.

Stone stood there for a full minute, wondering what
had just happened. Because he knew damned well that
something had. He had gone from teasing her—all right,
taunting her—to a bit of sexual innuendo. Had it been
harassment?

Well, hell—that was her game, not his. He had nothing to gain. And she had nothing to lose, he told himself. But because he was uncomfortable with the idea that
he had stepped over the bounds of decency, even though
common sense told him that a woman of her type was
probably used to that sort of thing, Stone deliberately
moved away from the pay phones.

He went inside and collected the Coronoke mail while
she placed her call. If she was calling a stringer for the
Atlanta Constitution, so be it. He wasn't going to hassle
her until he had something more to go on than a handful
of rumors and secondhand suspicions.

She was gone when he came outside, and he deliberately took his time getting to the marina. He refused to
believe it was his conscience bugging him, but something sure as hell was. Maybe he wasn't cut out for a life
of leisure. Maybe he'd spent too many years on the go—
following leads, tips, sometimes only hunches, sleeping
in tents, cargo planes, bomb shelters and noisy hotels.
This boondocks paradise was beginning to bug him. As

for the birds he was supposed to be watching, he had a feeling that by the time he left this place, the only kind of bird he'd want to see anytime soon would be a chicken. Preferably broiled.

That night, Stone sat on his deck under the yellow bug light and listened to the night noises, which included her guitar. She wasn't very good, but at least she had the decency to play quietly. If he'd thought to bring along a penny whistle, he might even have joined her. They were pretty much on an even level where musical ability was concerned. He was a gifted listener, period.

He'd picked up three newspapers over on Hatteras, but found he wasn't particularly interested in what was going on in the outside world. The latest from the Balkans, the latest from Congress, the latest from the royal family. Not to mention the perpetual mess in the Middle East.

Idly, he scratched the peeling sunburn on his shoulder and reached for Reece's letter again. He could still call him off. A trip back over to Hatteras. Or maybe Keegan's emergency radio channel could patch him through. But what the devil... he'd been increasingly restless this past week. Why not let the kid come on down? The way his ego was feeling at the moment, he could do with a touch of hero worship.

Lucy saw the light go on in the cottage through the woods. He was back. Was he reading, too? There was nowhere to go on this small, sparsely populated island, unless one visited the other cottagers. So far she hadn't. Had he?

The paperback romance lay unopened in her lap as she scratched idly at a mosquito bite. She was restless. She wasn't used to having time on her hands. The uneasy feeling that she was wasting time when she could be working to salt away something for a rainy day was inescapable. A rent-free summer vacation was all very well for those who could afford it, but second-year teachers didn't have a whole lot of job security.

With characteristic self-honesty, Lucy admitted that it wasn't a lack of job security, any more than it was a lack of activity, that was making her so edgy.

It was that man. That sanctimonious, acrimonious, binocular-toting...*bird-watcher!* How dare he look down his crooked nose at her? He didn't know her well enough to judge her.

But it was increasingly obvious that he had.

Well, she could judge, too, and from her point of view, Stone McCloud came up sadly lacking on all counts. The fact that he just happened to have the kind of looks she had always admired was irrelevant. Hamm Sheppard had had the same kind of wiry, lanky good looks—the same unruly dark hair and the same rugged, irregular kind of features. And he'd turned out to be a real jerk.

She had liked his family, though. The bald truth was, she had fallen in love with his family and probably would have married Hamm just so she could be a part of it, if she'd been old enough. And if Hamm hadn't scared the bejabbers out of her by trying to get her down in the back seat of his daddy's old Chevy. And if Pawpaw hadn't decided to pull up stakes and move down to Galveston right about then.

Feeling lonely and morose, Lucy wandered into the combination living-dining-room-kitchen and retrieved one of the candy bars she'd bought earlier. Maybe she should have bought a bottle of wine, but wine always made her sleepy. Besides, wine reminded her of Billy, who had been horrified the first time she'd brought home a jug of screw-top Chablis from the supermarket.

Munching chocolate and sipping diet cola, she opened her paperback romance and started reading about a heroine who had the strength, the brains and the courage to tackle the job of taming a surly protagonist, bringing out the best in him and creating a happy ending against overwhelming odds. *Sweet Tomorrows,* it was called.

A better title would have been *Fat Chance.*

Four

Jerry brought them over about five in the afternoon. Lucy heard them even before they erupted into the clearing. There were two adults and either four or five children. The way they moved, it was hard to count.

Maudie came next to open up the cottage and show them how things worked, and Lucy was waiting on the deck with two glasses of ice tea when she stopped in half an hour later.

"Here, you look as if you need this," she said, offering the cold drink.

"Funny... I don't remember children being so noisy. Ann Mary never was. Or is that something mothers conveniently forget, like labor pains?"

"As a schoolteacher, I can assure you that children are definitely noisy. Whoever suggested they could be seen and not heard evidently forgot to put the batteries in his hearing aid."

They laughed together and fell silent, but it was a comfortable silence. After a while, Maudie said she hoped Lucy's peace and quiet wasn't irretrievably shattered, and Lucy assured her that she could handle it. "I'm not sure I'm cut out for all this peace and quiet, after all. I teach sixth-graders, and there's a pair of eleven-month-old twins in the next apartment to mine."

"The Conners are the only family with young children scheduled until late July. This place seems to attract more singles and honeymooners—definitely not your average, run-of-the-mill summer vacationer."

The following morning Lucy met the Great American Novelist. He came out of his lair to complain about the noise just as she was walking past his cottage on her way to the swimming place. Evidently, the Conner crew had passed by only moments before.

"Are you one of them?" he demanded.

She looked him over before she replied. He was about sixty, hardly old enough to be such a Scrooge. Evidently, he worked at it. "One of the other cottagers? Yes, I'm in Heron's Rest."

"One of that gang of hoodlums that just raced past here."

"Gracious! Real hoodlums, here on Coronoke? The main reason I wanted to come here was because it was supposed to be so peaceful and safe. I'd better go back and lock all my doors and windows. Do you think we should—"

"Don't get smart with me, girly. You know blamed well who I'm talking about! That screaming bunch of brats that just streaked through my front yard."

There was no such thing as a yard at any of the Coronoke cottages. Each one was wedged in among the trees, near the beach and as much a part of the environment as it was possible for a man-made structure to be. Evidently, the man was territorial.

"You must mean the Conner children," Lucy said, forcing a smile. "They got in late yesterday evening— drove all the way from Indiana, I understand. I expect they'll blow off most of that energy in a day or so, but if you'd like, I'll speak to the parents."

He turned away, rubbing his grizzled beard. "No, no... never mind. Just— Who're you?"

This time, Lucy's smile didn't have to be forced. Why, the old fraud! "Lucy Dooley, from Winston-Salem... and parts south. I'm a schoolteacher. Who're you?"

He grunted, still not meeting her gaze. "*Harrumph!* Seymore. From Philly."

"It's nice to meet you, Mr. Seymore. I understand you're a writer?"

"A writer?" He frowned, but she wasn't fooled this time. She suspected he was all bluster on the outside and soft as a marshallow on the inside. Probably just shy.

"Maybe I misunderstood. When I first got here, Mrs. Keegan told me who my nearest neighbors were—the bird-watcher and the— I thought she said you were a novelist, but maybe I misunderstood. I was really bushed after driving all day to get here. That last leg by boat seemed to take forever."

Stone halted abruptly at the edge of the trees. Wearing black trunks, a pair of worn moccasins and a towel from the hotel where he'd recently resided, he'd been on his way to grab a swim before La Dooley came to do her laps. Evidently he was too late.

The bearded guy in the Hemingway getup must be the one Maudie had said was a writer. La Dooley hadn't wasted any time getting together with him. Stone made a silent decision to check the man out.

Dammit, just when he'd been about to think the charges against her were rigged, she had to go and pitch him a curve!

Lucy, unaware she was being observed, tried to draw Mr. Seymore out of his shell. There was something about him that reached out to her. According to Maudie, he used to come each year with his wife, who had died three years ago. Now he came alone each year, which struck her as terribly sad and beautiful. In a few days he'd be leaving, as lonely as he'd arrived, but before he did, Lucy vowed, she was going to get a smile out of him. One genuine smile.

"Mr. Seymore, have you seen the—"

A shrill whistle split the air and he turned to go inside, muttering something about a boiling kettle. Lucy gazed after him, idly scratching the rash on her hand that came from the scented dishwashing detergent she'd used. Some brands bothered her, some didn't. The one a previous tenant had left behind evidently did, which meant another trip to the market before she ran out of clean dishes.

"Pelicans?" she finished softly. Even Scrooge would have to smile at the pelicans. They were so wonderfully graceless.

On her way to the swimming place, Lucy frowned thoughtfully. She was almost sure Maudie had said he was a novelist—a writer of some sort. But then, he should certainly know.

Maybe he was a big-time crook hiding out from the law. Or an international spy, like the one in the book she'd just finished reading. Grinning, she loped the last few yards to the water and waded in, wishing the Conners had found another place to play, as they evidently weren't swimmers.

They were dog-paddlers, floaters, gigglers and splashers. Lucy managed to do three laps, but there was no way she could remain uninvolved once they hurled the ball her way. During the course of a no-holds-barred game of water polo, she came to know them all. Eleven-year-old Becky, ten-year-old Steve, seven-year-old Sara and six-year-old Mary. Evidently the Conners had had to pause between batches to catch their breath.

Later she met the parents, Paul and Edith. They were likable people, and Lucy ended up spending most of the day with them and the children on the beach.

More than once she found herself glancing around, looking for Stone McCloud. Irritated at her own weakness, she laughed just a little bit louder, played just a little bit harder and allowed the children to take advantage of her easygoing nature until she was near exhaustion.

"I can swim—watch me!" Becky cried.

She could dog-paddle. Almost. She definitely couldn't swim. Steve's form was only marginally better, and the two youngest couldn't even do that much.

Having lifeguarded and taught swimming practically all her adult life—it was a conveniently portable skill—Lucy found herself giving lessons until the sun was well on its way down. She was left alone on the beach with the children while Paul went to get the video camera and Edith started cooking supper.

Naturally, Lucy couldn't leave them unsupervised, so she stayed on until she was thoroughly tired, a bit chilly and had the beginnings of a headache.

Talk about a busman's holiday!

And then Paul came back with the camera, and she had to stay even longer to help the kids show off their marginal skills, holding chubby, earnest little Mary under the middle while she kicked and swatted water in her eyes.

"C'mon, kids, time to go ashore," she called out to a chorus of protests. Weak she might be, but Lucy was no pushover. "Out," she said firmly. "Chilled muscles cramp, and that means you won't be in any shape for another lesson tomorrow."

They trooped ashore, laughing and chattering, while Papa Conner, grinning and squinting, recorded it all for posterity.

"Hey, you were great," he said as she reached for the towel he held out in his free hand. "You're a natural with kids. Ought to have half a dozen or so of your own—talent like that shouldn't be wasted."

Lucy bent over from the waist and combed her fingers through her tangled hair, her face hidden. She no longer felt pain—not the raw, aching sense of loss she'd felt at first—but the scars would be with her for the rest of her life. For a long time after she had lost her baby, she had looked at every infant and thought, This could have been mine. Later on it had been toddlers, and even now she couldn't see a three-and-a-half-year-old without wondering....

Stone leaned up against the stunted hornbeam, his binoculars in one hand, watching her pick her way through the pine straw. He'd been checking on her throughout the afternoon, and he still didn't know what to think. He did know that Paul Conner was a senior staffer for an Indiana congressman and had come down to the Outer Banks with him once to stay at one of the VIP cottages the park service maintained. Pols were pols.

Or was he clutching at straws? Billy hadn't even made it in Georgia yet. He was a long way from Washington. Although Stone hadn't a doubt that that was where he had his sights set.

He continued to watch her approach, wincing for her when she stepped on a holly leaf. Even wet and obviously tired, her wild crop of hair frizzing around her head and her eyes red rimmed from too much saltwater, she had the power to sizzle a man's brain cells and send his libido into overdrive.

Damn. Why couldn't she have been a plain, dumpy frump with warts and an overbite?

But in that case, Billy would never have looked at her twice, let alone married her. And Stone wouldn't be here, watching and wondering, his suspicions alternately rising and falling.

She still hadn't noticed him. To anyone coming in off the beach, the woods were dark and shadowy. Telling himself he was merely observing—a good journalist always observed carefully before he took a position—he watched her make her way along the path. Words formed in his head. Phrases like *walking fantasy* and *deceptive look of innocence.* Tousled hair, sleepy eyes, long, golden limbs and a way of walking that hit a man square in the solar plexus . . . and then dropped lower.

He hadn't bargained on having to deal with all that.

Not until she was only a few yards away did he step away from the gnarled trunk of the hornbeam. "Hi. Been doing your laps?"

Lucy jumped. One hand flew up to her breast. "Stone! You scared the daylights out of me! I didn't see you standing there. What were you doing—watching a bird?"

"Yeah. He just flew away, though."

"Sorry if I scared him. What was it?"

Stone fell in beside her. "Brown-speckled snuff dipper. They're rare in these parts."

She walked silently for a minute, picking her way carefully through squirrel-chewed pinecone scales. Then she cut him a suspicious look. "A *what?*"

"You being a city woman, you probably never even heard of them."

"No, but I've heard of the forked-tongue tale spinner. In fact, I think I just heard one."

"No kidding. Was it the mating call?" Stone quipped, responding instinctively to the laughter dancing in her pink-rimmed eyes.

"More like the battle call." Her stomach rumbled noisily. "Now that, I do believe, was the chow call of the yellow-crested stilt." She laughed, and his deep chuckle joined in. It was a surprisingly companionable sound.

They approached Mr. Seymore's cottage, and Lucy held a finger to her lips for silence. Once past, Stone caught her by the arm, his brows lifted questioningly.

"He hates noise. The Conner kids drove him wild, but I don't think he's nearly as bad as he pretends to be. I expect that crust he wears is just a defense. Maudie said he was some kind of a writer. A widower."

Which could mean anything or nothing, Stone mused. He would bear watching, but it was the Conner guy who worried him most.

"How well do you know Paul Conner?" he asked just as they came abreast of his own cottage. She kept on walking. So did Stone.

"Not very well." She sent him a curious look. "Nice children."

"I noticed you went out of your way to ingratiate yourself with them."

She halted. "To what?"

"Poor choice of words," he said. "You let them walk all over you. Do you usually do that?"

"Splash all over me, maybe. No one walks all over me. And no, I don't."

He figured it was about time to change subjects. "Look, I ordered a few pounds of shrimp when Keegan went over for mail this morning, but now that I've got the critters, I'm not quite sure what to do with them. Can you eat 'em raw, like oysters?"

"You can eat anything raw if you've got the nerve, but these days, I wouldn't recommend it. I'll write you out an easy recipe if you want. Are they headed or not?"

"Gee, I don't know." He raked a hand through his shaggy near-black hair, and Lucy found herself wanting to replace his fingers with her own. His hair looked surprisingly soft. He was about two weeks overdue for a trim, and on him, it looked good. On him, everything looked good—even those cool, watchful gray eyes of his.

"Let me get changed and I'll go back with you and see. If they're already headed, I'll put them on to boil for you, seasoning and all. All you'll have to do is take them up, peel them and eat them."

The shrimp were already headed. In the end, they both peeled and both ate. It took nearly an hour, and after spending practically all day in the water swimming, playing and teaching, Lucy was famished. She'd put the shrimp on to simmer in salt water and vinegar, adding black pepper, two cloves, a slice of lemon and a cluster of wax myrtle leaves from the bush outside. She would've used filé powder if she'd had it, the way Lillian had taught her, but it would be almost as good without.

While she measured rice into a pan and set it to cooking, Stone made a salad using ingredients she would never have thought of combining. He was nothing if not daring. Fortunately, she was hungry enough to overlook sauerkraut and canned string beans in her salad.

When the shrimp were done, she drained off all but a bit of broth and lifted out the shrimp, and they both peeled, laughing when the juice dripped down their arms. More than once she glanced up to find Stone's puzzled gaze on her.

"What's the matter? Do I have a bit of shell stuck to my face?" she asked the third time she caught him staring at her.

"No, I— What? It's for real, isn't it? Your hair?"

"No, it's excelsior," she said with a straight face. "They used to use it for packing stuff in until some fruitcake invented plastic peanuts. The poor excelsior people were about to go out of business, so I invented excelsior wigs. Chic, huh?" She pretended to preen while shrimp juice dripped down her forearms.

"Cute," Stone said dryly.

"Well, you don't think anyone would deliberately choose hair like this, do you?" Her brown eyes teased, her full lips parted, revealing a row of white, slightly irregular teeth. Stone found himself dangerously close to losing his perspective.

Slowly, Lucy's smile faded. She sighed. What was it with this man? One minute he was teasing her, and the next it was almost as if the sun had gone behind a cloud. Gathering up her newspapers full of peelings and trimmings, she was looking for a place to put them when Stone removed the bundle from her hands.

"I'll take care of these. Through there if you want to wash up." He nodded to one of several doors leading off the living-dining area and Lucy realized that, although the decor was different, the layout of Hawk's Nest was identical to that of Heron's Rest.

"What I need is about three days in a bathtub," she said ruefully, peeling a segment of shrimp shell off the back of her arm.

"Be my guest."

But his gray eyes were back to semiglacial again, and Lucy shook her head. "Thanks. I guess I can make do with a lick and a promise."

She soaped her arms all the way up to her elbows and beyond, trying not to look at the scant array of masculine toiletries and the plume of wild grass someone had rammed into the toothbrush glass. Fortunately, he didn't go in for scented soaps. After rinsing her arms and splashing water over her face, she dampened her hair and tried to press it closer to her scalp.

Excelsior just about described it! She was going to whack the stuff off right up to her scalp the minute she got back home! Sooner, if she could borrow a pair of scissors.

When she returned, looking damp and smelling clean and wholesome in a way that he found oddly intriguing, Stone had dressed the salad and was just pouring the wine. Her cheeks were flushed, he noticed.

Her eyes had that soft, sultry look he was coming to expect from her, even when she was ticked off. Which, where he was concerned, was more often than not, he thought ruefully.

"You're sunburned," he observed.

"I never burn. If I'm pink, it comes from being steamed."

"Was it something I said?" he inquired innocently.

"Probably," she drawled, her sultry voice spiced by a touch of laughter.

Lucy added a blob of butter to the small amount of broth left in the shrimp pot, then dumped the shrimp back in to reheat before pouring the succulent pink concoction over a bed of steaming rice. Glancing up, she observed, "If anyone's sunburned, it's you. And don't tell me it's all from bending over a hot salad bowl."

But it was neither a hot salad bowl nor a hot stove she was bending over at the moment. As she leaned over to place the platter in the center of the table, Stone gazed his fill at the soft cotton wraparound skirt that molded her firm backside in a way that made the palms of his hands jealous.

The meal was simple, but superb. The tension that had arisen so suddenly was defused by the ordinary business of feeding another kind of hunger. They fought over the last shrimp, ended up splitting it, and Lucy scraped the last grain of rice from the platter while Stone opened a second bottle of wine. "Don't—not for me," she protested just as the cork came out with a vaporous sigh. "I never drink." She'd already had two glasses.

"Celebration," he replied, filling her glass again.

"What are we celebrating?" Lucy told herself she wasn't tipsy. A bit fizzy, maybe, but not really tipsy. The rice absorbed any excess alcohol—hadn't she read that somewhere?

"We could drink to the armistice," he said in a silky tone that she didn't quite trust.

Or wouldn't have trusted, if it hadn't been for the fizz in her brain. "Which armistice is that?"

"Ours. Three and a half hours together without a single cross word."

Well, naturally she couldn't refuse to toast the fall of the Stone wall. Clinking her glass against his, she made an effort to keep her eyelids from slipping any lower. Wine always made her eyelids grow heavy.

There was no dishwasher. Stone insisted on leaving the dishes, and Lucy was in no mood to argue. About anything.

He led her out onto the deck, and somehow they wound up discussing—of all things—allergies. She complimented him on his toilet soap and told him about being allergic to dishwashing detergent, and he recommended wearing gloves. Which she did, of course—at home.

"How did we get on this subject?" she asked, meaning how could any woman in her right mind, finding herself alone with an attractive man in a romantic setting, be so gauche as to talk about rashes and itches?

His face in shadow, Stone watched her. She intrigued him. He would have expected her to start coming on to him by now. According to Alice, she'd been after anything in pants, and what he'd seen so far seemed to bear it out.

Except for the children. That didn't fit the profile.

"Shall we talk about the moonlight on the water? Or about our first time?"

"First time for what?" Absently, she dug at a mosquito bite on her thigh. Finding no satisfaction in scratching through two layers of cotton, she flipped the overlap of her wraparound aside and got to the heart of the matter. "Do you remember when you had chicken pox?" she asked.

"Chicken pox?"

"Everyone has chicken pox. I've just discovered that mosquito bites are a lot like chicken pox, only the itch lasts longer."

Curiouser and curiouser. The woman was either smarter than he'd given her credit for being, or he was baby-sitting the wrong female. There couldn't be two Lucy Dooleys—not on Coronoke. "How about measles?"

She shook her head. "That's different. If you'd ever had measles, you'd know it. Everything that doesn't itch aches. You feel really lousy."

He'd had measles the year he'd gone off to military school. At Christmas. Alone except for the sour-faced infirmary nurse, he'd thought life couldn't get any worse. He'd been wrong.

"I had 'em," he said. "What about mumps? You ever have those?"

"When I was four and a half. You?"

"When I was five. Fortunately. How about scarlet fever?"

"I don't think so. Let me see, we were living with Lillian when I had measles. I think we were living in a boarding house in Pascagoula when I had mumps. The woman next door looked after me during the day. We were with Ollie Mae in Galveston when I had my tonsils out, and I don't remember coming down with anything when we lived with Geneva, so I guess I must have missed scarlet fever."

"Dare I ask who Lillian and Ollie Mae and Geneva were? It sounds as if you moved around a lot."

"They were some of Paw—my father's mistresses. And yes, we did move around a lot."

Stone finished his wine and carefully set the glass on the railing. Outside, even as the moon rose in the east, a glimmer of vermillion still showed in the Western sky. A chuck-will's-widow piped up from the nearby woods, and from the water came the splash of a jumping mullet.

In spite of certain misgivings, a deep sense of peace began to seep into his body, into his mind. He sighed and closed his eyes, wondering how he could feel so contented in the presence of a woman who was supposed to be the enemy. This wasn't smart, he told himself. Letting her sneak under his defenses this way. The first thing any good journalist had to learn was to maintain his objectivity—how else could he do his job? No bias, no personal agenda, no ax to grind.

Objectivity? If he'd ever had any, it was shot all to hell and gone. He sighed again, wishing he had a cigarette, even though he'd quit smoking several years ago. "I'd better get those dishes in soaking," he said, wondering if a man could ever call himself a man again after he'd used dishwashing as an excuse to distance himself from a desirable woman.

What was that cliché? Any old port in a storm?

Any old excuse when a man was in danger of making a monumental blunder.

As the effects of several glasses of wine began to wear off, warning lights were flashing on in his mind. He was entirely too comfortable. Entirely too satisfied.

At least, some parts of him were satisfied.

The truth was, he was entirely too close to falling under the spell of the very woman he'd been sent here to spy on.

He watched her stand up and place her glass beside his on the railing. That was another thing—that way she had of standing slightly pigeon-toed. Deliberately trying to confuse him.

Alice Hardisson's words came back to him. "Perfectly awful woman... A tramp named Lucy Dooley... No more sense of how to go on than a stray cat. All that hair and those cheap clothes—"

Tramp like Lucy Dooley. Tramp like Lucy Dooley....

The words echoed in his mind, becoming tangled with Lillian and Ollie Mae, with Paw and measles and children's laughter on the beach.

Who *was* Lucy Dooley?

What the hell was she doing here?

And what the devil was he going to do about her?

Five

The Conner children were at Lucy's cottage before she'd even had her breakfast. Cheerfully resigned, she turned off the burner under her corned-beef hash and invited them inside while she got dressed.

"Mama said we shouldn't make pests of ourselves," Becky said anxiously. "We had breakfast two hours ago. What's that stuff in the frying pan?"

"You're not making pests of yourselves," Lucy assured them. "I slept late because I stayed up to finish a book." She'd read for an hour or so, but it had been the dreams—more vivid, more intense than any she had ever experienced—that had wakened her and left her lying there in the middle of the night, unable to go back to sleep until just before dawn. "As for that stuff in the pan, it's something my daddy used to cook for breakfast when I was a little girl."

She could have used another few hours of privacy to get over the effects of those heated dreams, but a few hours of noisy, uncomplicated activity was probably a better antidote.

"I heard a whippoorwill last night," Steve confided. He was eyeing her guitar case with a look that made Lucy groan inwardly. Swimming lessons were one thing. Music lessons were quite another.

Musically, she was barely qualified to play, much less to teach.

"I think it might have been a chuck-will's-widow. Listen again tonight and see if you can tell the difference."

Someone rapped on the open door, and the same dusky voice that had haunted her dreams all night said calmly, "I've got a book on birds if you're interested, son. Good morning, Ms. Dooley."

"Her name's not Miz Dooley, it's Lucy," piped Sara. "She told us we could call her that, didn't you, Lucy?"

Stone didn't miss the proprietary tone of voice. With a lift of one dark eyebrow he conveyed his amusement to Lucy, and then he sniffed. "Hmm...smells interesting in here."

"My breakfast."

"Cinnamon toast, right?"

As the house was permeated with the smell of fried onions, Lucy ignored the remark. Sliding the covered pan into the refrigerator, she tied her skirt over the bathing suit she'd put on after her morning shower and gathered up a towel, a pair of sunglasses and a slightly shriveled apple. Then she poured herself a mug of thick, chicory-flavored coffee. The hash could wait. "Okay, who's ready for a swimming lesson?"

To a loud chorus of *me's* and *I am's,* she hustled her young friends out the door. Stone turned to follow, the look of amusement broadening into a grin as he murmured something about pied pipers.

It occurred to Lucy that if he had happened to tune in on her dreams last night, he might not be feeling quite so complaisant. Probably be halfway to Hatteras by now, because unless she was very much mistaken, Stone McCloud was that stock character found in all the best romances and men's adventure stories—a loner.

In which case, she'd better not be having any more dreams like the one she'd had last night—dreams that had her heart pounding, her bones melting and her arms aching to hold something more solid than a feather pillow.

They swam until noon, and then Lucy begged off to go make her bed and reheat her breakfast for lunch. Stone had disappeared after the first hour or so, having lingered on the beach for a while to talk to Paul Conner.

The children gobbled down their sandwiches in record time and were at her door, ready to escort her back to the beach, before she had finished her lunch, but she went cheerfully. She'd always found children to be good company. It was the fathers who occasionally complicated matters. Not that Paul had shown the least interest beyond simple friendliness, but she was wary all the same, having been put in an embarrassing position more than once.

But it wasn't Paul Conner who made the skin prickle on the back of her neck as she followed the children along the path to the swimming area. It was a certain birdwatcher. A lean, cool-eyed stranger who had a way of moving that redefined all she had ever learned about the anatomy of the male. A man who made her feel about as secure as a fledgling being watched by a hovering hawk.

A man who was essentially a loner, she reminded herself forcefully as the four Conners ran ahead and belly flopped, and then yelled for her to come save them.

Mr. Seymore was on his deck when she passed by late that afternoon, exhausted from her daylong romp with the young Conners. He greeted her warily, and she responded with a broad, answering smile and a few words about the likelihood of rain. When he only grunted and disappeared inside, Lucy shrugged. Rome wasn't built in a day.

Of Stone, she saw little. A day passed, and then another. She tried not to admit, even to herself, that she missed him, because admitting that would be admitting her own vulnerability.

But she did. And she was. Stone McCloud was excellent company when he wanted to be. He could also be surly as a dog with a four-alarm toothache, and there was no way of predicting which mood he was going to be in.

If she had any brains, she would leave him to his birds.

Maudie dropped by to leave a letter from Frank, with notes enclosed from both his daughters. Frank's handwriting wasn't quite as legible as Amy's, and only marginally clearer than Muffy's crayoned scrawl. He had remembered to water her violets. The rain had stopped, and he'd aired her place out, but her kitchen drawers still wouldn't quite shut. Amy was playing a Chopin piece in the class recital. Muffy had lost another tooth.

Lucy sighed, the letters falling unheeded to the floor. She missed them all so much....

Didn't she?

Well, of course she missed them. They were friends, as well as neighbors. For a little while she'd thought they might even become something more, but she knew now it would never have worked. Frank was a wonderful man, and the girls were precious, but once was enough. One bad marriage and a few near misses were more than enough to teach her that getting emotionally involved with any man simply wasn't worth the risk.

Besides, there was no reason why a woman couldn't be perfectly happy with a satisfying career, a comfortable place to call home and a few really good friends. Although *content* might be a better term than *happy*. And as for the home, there was room for improvement on that score, too.

At least she made friends easily. It was a skill she'd been forced to cultivate, moving around so much in her early life.

Pity she didn't do as well with lovers.

The Conners and Mr. Seymore were scheduled to leave on Sunday morning. Lucy made a point of being on hand to say goodbye, receiving hugs and kisses from the girls, a snort and a look of embarrassment from Steve and heartfelt thanks from Edith and Paul for all the time she had spent with the children.

Ignoring them all, Mr. Seymore brushed past to climb stiffly down into the Keegans' red runabout, clutching a small suitcase and a briefcase. No typewriter, Lucy noticed. So much for the Great American Novel.

But she was still determined to get that smile. Moving closer, she said quietly, "Mr. Seymore, you owe me for keeping the hoodlums at bay."

"Owe you! I don't owe nobody nothing, girly!" he snorted.

"What hoodlums?" Steve demanded. "I didn't see any hoodlums on Coronoke. Nobody ever tells me anything!"

"I know what a hoodalum is. It's that big bird that carries fish in its beak," Mary said smugly.

The throng on the pier needed only Stone to be complete. By the time he made it down to see what all the commotion was about, there was scarcely room for one more.

"That's a pelican, silly," said Becky. "Mr. McCloud's book said so, didn't it, Mr. McCloud? There's no such bird as a hoodalum, is there?"

That was when Lucy got her wish. Mr. Seymore smiled. It was a stiff one, granted, and it lasted only a moment, but it was real while it lasted. "Hoodlum," he muttered. "That's a good one!"

There was another round of hugs, and then Lucy knelt on the edge of the pier and beckoned to the gray-bearded recluse. "Oh, Mr. Seymore, you forgot something."

With a suspicious look, he stood and leaned closer. Lucy quickly wrapped her arms around his neck and whispered, "You forgot to hug me goodbye."

She could have sworn he blushed. Maudie grinned. The others were too busy to notice. All except Stone, who wore his usual look of cool disapproval.

So what else was new? she thought. At least she'd gotten her smile. One of the early lessons life had taught her was that when large victories were scarce on the ground, a frugal person made do with small ones.

Rich cast off the stern line and turned to clasp his wife's shoulders. Even in paint-stained khakis and a faded red T-shirt, he looked severe and military. "You go home and take a nap now, you hear? Set one foot on that ladder and I'll nail your hide to the boathouse wall."

"Oh, how lovely! No nap, darling, but I promise you, no ladders, either."

He muttered something about insubordination. "Okay, then lie down and read a book. Read two books. Hell, watch the mullet jump, I don't care. Just promise me you won't get into any trouble while I'm gone, will you do that?"

Lucy felt an absurd urge to weep at the unselfconscious display of domineering tenderness. Every woman should be so lucky!

The Conner kids were squabbling over who sat where. When Rich began to hand out life vests, they assured him they didn't have to wear them because Lucy had taught them to swim.

"Yeah, I know, but humor me, will you? I don't want the Coast Guard on my case. They get real sticky about their rules."

"It's going to seem awfully quiet around here for the next few days," Lucy murmured. Watching Stone leaning against the boathouse, arms crossed over his chest, she wondered what it would feel like to have a husband who couldn't bear to part with her for even an hour without making a major deal of it.

Because Maudie looked so wistful, Lucy made an attempt to distract her. "By the way, speaking of reading, Mr. Seymore claims he's not a writer. What do you suppose he really does?"

It was Keegan who supplied the answer. "Seymore? He's in the insurance business. What made you think he was a—"

Lucy looked at Maudie. Maudie looked at Lucy. They both began to laugh at the same time. "An underwriter!" Maudie gasped.

"So that's why you thought—"

Stone looked at them both as if they'd lost their minds, and as the boat pulled away from the pier, leaving the three of them behind, Lucy waved one last time. "Just goes to show you that things aren't always what they seem to be," she said, turning away.

A full head shorter than her companion, Maudie trudged alongside. "Sorry if I misled you. I'm not playing with a full deck these days. Sometimes I think my body's been invaded by aliens." She grinned. "In fact, I know it has."

That night, Rich Keegan came to Lucy's cottage after she'd gone to bed. She was reading. The light was still on, and at first she thought it might be Stone. She'd been half expecting to see him all day, but evidently he had better things to do.

"Lucy, I hate to bother you, but Maudie's having some pretty bad cramps. I've talked to the doctor—I'm picking him up at the marina in half an hour, but I don't want to leave her alone. Can you come?"

Hurriedly, Lucy flung her wraparound skirt on over the T-shirt she slept in. *Oh, Lord, please let her be all right! Please don't take her baby, too!* "Has she had any trouble before now?"

Rich said she hadn't, but Lucy could tell he was worried sick. She didn't blame him. She was worried, too. She would have worried about any woman in those circumstances, but she'd grown fond of Maudie Keegan even in the short time she'd known her.

"Of course I'll be glad to stay with her, but I don't know what I can do if—"

Rich's intensely blue eyes darkened to navy, and she silently reproached herself. She could stay calm, for starters. "A few stomach cramps don't necessarily mean anything," she said. "It's probably just indigestion. What did she eat for supper?"

Rich had grabbed her hand and was practically dragging her along behind him. "Supper? Oh—uh, baked flounder. Some kind of green stuff. Cornbread and about half a jar of fig preserves. She likes figs."

"It's probably just gas pains," Lucy said, praying she was right. These two didn't deserve this kind of grief. No one deserved the grief of losing a child.

In an effort to distract him, she said, "I've heard of house calls, Rich, but *island calls?* You two must have some real clout."

Rich shook his head. "God, I hope so! If you've got any pull upstairs, we could use a good word." He was crushing her fingers in his big, hard hand, but not for the world would Lucy have complained. She was glad, however, that she had taken the time to step into her loafers. Just past Hawk's Nest, he led them off the path, plunging into the woods along a shortcut that had been only marginally cleared. Neither of them noticed the silent figure standing in the doorway of the nearby cottage.

Stone watched the shadowy figures, hand in hand, disappear into the woods. He swore silently, fists clenched at his sides.

Maudie was paler than usual—at least, Lucy thought she was. Under the artificial light, it was hard to say with any certainty, but her cheerfulness was patently forced.

"I told him I didn't need a baby-sitter," she said by way of greeting. Fully dressed, she was lying on the sofa, an unopened book on her lap.

"I needed something to do now that the gang's all gone. Did you see Mr. Seymore smile today? I promised myself I'd get a smile out of that man before he left, and I did."

Rich cut into their small talk. "You're not to get up for anything short of an earthquake, is that clear?" he ordered. Lucy was busy checking her bare legs for crawling insects.

Maudie crossed her arms over her chest. "Aren't you being a little bit foolish about a few stomach pains?"

"Call it what you will, but you try to get up off that couch before I get back and Lucy has orders to sit on you."

"I do?" Lucy murmured.

"You do," the tall ex-air-force colonel said firmly.

After he'd gone, Lucy made them both mugs of strong tea, adding milk and sugar to both. Maudie thanked her and apologized for bothering her in the middle of the night, and they began to talk. About men, about husbands, about childhoods and children.

For differing reasons, they never got around to discussing pregnancy.

Stone heard the runabout leave the pier. His mood darkened from an already stygian blackness. The little slut! Why Keegan, of all men? With a single man available, why pick on a married one? He'd thought he was a pretty good judge of character, but evidently he'd been reading Keegan all wrong.

As for Lucy, she'd almost managed to convince him that Alice had been mistaken about her. Things weren't always what they seemed to be. Where had he heard that recently?

But then, sometimes things were precisely what they seemed.

Quietly furious, Stone heard the boat return about forty-five minutes later. Evidently they hadn't gone far.

Just far enough out so that they could be assured of a little privacy.

He had opened a beer and left it untouched on the railing. Earlier, he'd poured himself a glass of wine and then ignored that, too. What he really wanted was a stiff belt of whiskey, the rawer the better.

But what he needed was a clear head.

She came back alone. The bastard didn't even have the class to see her safely back to her cottage. But then, between the pair of them, there wasn't a whole lot of class to spare.

Stone was waiting on her deck when she came inside. He'd wanted to face them together, intending to spell out a few home truths about the kind of men who had it all and still weren't satisfied.

By this time he'd built up a fine head of steam.

"Satisfied?" he asked silkily. *It's none of your business, man. Let it go!*

Startled, Lucy dropped the shoes she'd just emptied of sand and pine straw. "Stone? What on earth are you doing here? You scared the dickens out of me!"

"What's the matter? Don't tell me your conscience is getting to you."

"My— I don't know what you're talking about."

"No, of course you don't. Women like you don't have a conscience, do they? Might get in the way of your sleazy little life-style."

"You've been drinking, haven't you?" She knew about men and alcohol. Her father had been a cheerful drinker, buying drinks for all his friends and gifts for all his women, even when they'd been dead flat broke, and only rarely getting into fights—which was fortunate, because he invariably lost.

Billy turned mean as a snake—and twice as unpredictable—when he drank too much. He liked to fight, but only when he was sure his opponent was no match for him.

Stone was evidently one of those men who turned suspicious with one drink too many.

"As it happens," he said very quietly, "I'm sober. Too damn sober, but that's irrelevant."

Lucy edged toward the inner door, wishing—hoping—that this would turn out to be just another wild dream. It was nearly three in the morning. After the doctor had pronounced Maudie's cramps to be of the nonthreatening variety, she had offered to stay on while Rich returned him to Hatteras. But by then, Maudie was in her bed, sleeping soundly. She had walked with Rich and the doctor through the woods until the path had split off to go down to the pier, assuring them that she could go the rest of the way alone. A full moon rode high overhead, making even the woods passably bright.

Of course, she'd had no way of knowing she would find a madman lurking on her own front deck. "I think you'd better leave," she said with all the quiet dignity she could muster.

"What's the matter, are you too tired to entertain another man tonight?"

She didn't know what he was implying—or why—but she did recognize an insult when she heard one. "Stone, whatever you came here to discuss, can it wait until morning? I'm tired, and you're obviously not yourself."

"Tired? A big party girl like you? I should have thought you'd just be hitting your stride about now."

The muffled roar of the Keegan's runabout came clearly through the still night air. Stone turned toward the sound. Lucy had almost reached the door when he caught her by the arm and swung her around.

"What the hell's going on around here?" he demanded, his voice rough edged, threatening.

"Please take your hand off my arm," she said very quietly.

"I asked you—"

"And I told you!"

"Dammit, woman!" He jerked her around, slamming her body hard against his. Before she could move away, his arms came around her, clamping her there with merciless strength. There was no hint at all of the cool and impersonal bird-watcher in the man who grasped the back of her head in one hand, tangling his fingers in her hair until he had positioned her to his liking.

Nothing at all cool and impersonal in the lips that crushed her own, twisting to gain entrance. He was surprisingly strong. Lucy was no weakling. Years of swimming had seen to that, but she was no match for the man who held her.

At first, shock held her captive, and then, even as she gathered herself to push him forcefully away, his hold eased, the kiss changed imperceptibly into something more persuasive. His hand curved around the back of her head and his mouth lifted, and he whispered her name. "Lucy. Lucy..."

She could easily have broken away. Instead, she stood stiffly in his embrace, her heart aching as if it had shattered into a million pieces.

Which was, of course, absurd.

Slowly Stone released her. His fingers trailed from her waist and her hair, one finger lingering to caress her cheek. A beam of moonlight fell across the side of his face, illuminating the irregularity of his rugged features, leaving his expression in shadow.

"Is that it? May I go inside now?" Her voice was thready, but she clung to her dignity, head held high and spine erect.

Stone's hands fell to his sides. He stepped back, swore once and then turned and left. Lucy didn't know whether to cry or to throw a shoe at him.

Lacking the energy to do either, she went inside and fell across her bed. She could cry tomorrow, when she didn't feel quite so raw. If that didn't help, she might try throwing a few pieces of porch furniture at him.

Six

___

Surprisingly enough, Lucy slept soundly. She woke with the sun in her eyes, groaned and pulled a pillow over her head. It was hot in the small bedroom in spite of the ceiling fan and four open windows. The Coronoke cottages, with their individual generators, didn't run to air conditioners. That in itself was no real hardship. Lucy had grown up with ceiling fans, electric floor fans—even paddle-handled cardboard ones, usually advertising a local mortuary. She still harbored fond memories of sitting on the porch swing and fanning herself with Rebecca-at-the-well while Lillian shelled butter beans.

Groaning, she sat up. First order of the day: shower, twist up her hair into as many ponytails as it took to keep it off her neck and put together something for breakfast.

Second order of the day: find something to occupy all the hours between now and bedtime so that she wouldn't have time to think about what had happened last night. Or wonder why it had happened.

Lucy knew all about pheromones. She had studied biology. She had been married, for pity sake, and if all that weren't educational enough, she'd had years of seeing the effect her father had had on women—and the effect women had had on him.

One of her old anthropology teachers had summed it up concisely, if none too encouragingly. From time immemorial, some women, either consciously or unconsciously, cast out lures. And some men reacted to those lures like carp to a stink bait. Hormones being what they were, the inevitable happened. Testosterone surged. Men got aggressive. Women conceived. Men pulled on their loincloth and went about their business, leaving the woman to deal with the inevitable consequences.

Thousands of years later, some things were pretty much the same. The only thing that had changed was that women had gotten smarter.

Correction. *Some* women had gotten smarter. If Lucy had been casting any subconscious lures in Stone's direction—and she wouldn't deny the possibility—then at least she had sense enough now to know the risks.

Was he worth it?

Common sense said one thing. Instinct said another.

Lucy raked her fingers through her damp hair. She turned the ceiling fan up a notch and allowed the breeze to cool her overheated body. Absently, she chewed on a ragged nail she had broken while trying to pry open a package of flashlight batteries. The thing snagged on everything, and she really didn't need the additional aggravation.

Her fitted leather manicure kit was one Alice had given her for Christmas the first year she'd been married. Up until then, an emery board and a pair of nail clippers had served the purpose. This luxury model held tools she still hadn't figured out a use for.

Such as three pairs of scissors, one with curved blades, one with blunt-tipped blades and one with blades almost two inches long.

Twenty minutes later, Lucy stood in front of the bathroom mirror and examined the results of her handiwork. One thing about naturally curly hair—cropped short enough, it was a lot more forgiving of amateur bungling than straight hair would have been. Considering the fact that she had probably saved herself about twenty bucks, it looked darned good! At least her face showed now—although she wasn't altogether sure that was a blessing.

She was sitting on a small cypress table on the front deck after breakfast, experimenting with the chording of an old Cajun melody, when Stone walked up from the shore. Her fingers slid dissonantly over the strings, and she stared through the screen. "What do you want?" she challenged when he stopped just outside her screen door.

The jeans he was wearing were bleached almost white—by nature, not by any fancy acid-bleaching, stone-washing technique. His faded khaki shirt hung open halfway down to reveal a strip of skin that was faintly pink under a thicket of dark chest hair. The tip of his crooked nose was pink, too. In fact, he looked almost as if he were blushing from the neck down.

"May I come in?" he asked.

"I'd rather you didn't. I'm busy."

His gaze dropped to the scarred guitar that lay across her lap. "I see. I heard you playing."

"So? I don't charge admission."

"Good. You'd starve if you did."

"You're a music critic? I knew you were a critic, I just wasn't sure what kind," she said sweetly.

"I'm not a music critic, but I'm not tone-deaf, either."

"Well, bully for you," she snapped, wishing she could think of a devastating response. Or even an intelligent one. She'd always had a quick temper. The trouble was, her brain usually lagged about three paces behind her tongue.

"Look, I didn't come by to talk about music. I—"

"Good. Then I won't keep you."

"I came by to apologize."

Her back grew inches taller. Her head came up perceptibly. "Oh? For which offense? I'll need to know to keep my records straight."

Stone jerked open the screen and came inside, radiating anger, frustration and some intangible energy that had Lucy holding her breath until she thought her lungs would burst. "Don't be so damned hard-nosed, woman. You know whi— What the hell have you done to yourself?"

He stared at her, and Lucy knew a moment of deep satisfaction. "I beg your pardon?"

"You know what I mean!" He pointed at her hair, his eyes hot with accusation. "What happened to your head?"

"My head or my hair? I really don't see how that concerns you, but since you asked, I gave myself a trim. I should think that was fairly obvious. Incidentally, you could really do with a haircut yourself. If you get much shaggier you're going to have to braid it."

"We're not talking about me, we're talking about you! What the devil got into you?"

He was standing so close, the soft denim of his jeans brushed her bare knee. Invading her personal space. It wasn't the first time, but this time was different. Lucy felt threatened, and for the life of her, she didn't know why. Even when he had forcibly kissed her, she had sensed that he wasn't the kind of man who would hurt her physically. He wasn't like Billy. In spite of his surly disposition, she knew intuitively that Stone wasn't hiding a broad streak of viciousness behind a polished facade, the way Billy had. For one thing, he lacked the polished facade.

All the same, every time he touched her—every time he even came near her—she felt as if all the insulation had been suddenly stripped from her nerves. Another allergy to contend with, she thought with bitter amusement. She really needed that!

Standing abruptly, she moved to put the table between them, holding her guitar in front of her as if it was a shield. "Look," she said huskily, "I don't know why you're apologizing, and I don't know why you got so upset last night, but I do know that I can live without the hassle. If that's all you wanted to say, then consider it said." Only a few inches shorter than he was, she looked him directly in the eye, wondering distractedly how she could ever have thought gray eyes were cold. She swallowed hard. "So, now, if you don't mind, I've got dishes to wash."

Stone watched in helpless anger as she turned and stalked off into the cottage. She didn't shut the door between them. He could have followed, but that would only have made things worse. He still didn't know what had happened between her and Keegan last night. He might never know. He did know that he'd wakened this morning after a lousy night feeling as if the ground under his feet had tilted a few degrees off true.

Stone had learned a long time ago that things weren't always drawn in black-and-white. Nothing was so simple. There was an infinite variety of grays out there, and grays were a hell of a lot tougher to judge. Yet there were times when a guy had no choice but to make a judgment call. Without judgments, there could be no standards, and without standards, things quickly deteriorated into chaos. God knows, he'd seen firsthand what could happen when the basic tenets of civilization were ignored.

He had decided to withhold judgment for the time being, which meant he owed her an apology. A conditional apology, subject to withdrawal if his suspicions proved correct. But things hadn't gone exactly the way he'd planned, and somehow he had ended up on the defensive.

Back to the drawing board.

Over the next few days, Stone found one excuse after another to seek out Lucy's company. He sat in the shade of the woods while she swam laps, so he could walk back to the cottage with her. She sauntered along beside him, looking like an advertisement for summer, with her tall, big-boned body, her silky, tanned skin and her golden halo of curls.

She didn't invite him inside her cottage. He invited her to go with him while he made a supply run to Hatteras, but she declined, giving him a cool little smile that drove him right out of his gourd.

Dammit, she was screwing up his professional objectivity!

The very first time he had laid eyes on Lucy Dooley, she'd gotten under his skin. And that was plain nuts! He had come down here, despising in principle everything she stood for, and all primed to take her apart. Instead, she had disarmed him again and again by stepping out of character. Every time he thought he had her pegged, she pulled her chameleon act and he was right back where he'd started, wondering if the crack on his head had permanently rearranged his brain.

Either he was losing his edge, or she wasn't the greedy, unprincipled witch he'd been sent down here to keep under wraps.

Was she on the level? Or was she just an exceptional actress? And if she was on the level, then what did that say about his aunt? God knows, Stone had no great love for the woman who had taken him in out of a chilly sense of obligation all those years ago and then proceeded to ignore him in all but the most perfunctory way, but at least he had always respected her. Women of Alice Hardisson's stamp had integrity bred into the marrow of their bones, while women like Lucy Dooley...

That was the trouble. Stone didn't really know any women like Lucy Dooley. He was beginning to think she was one of a kind.

In spite of all common sense—in spite of her personal experience with men—Lucy was intrigued by her laconic bird-watching neighbor. Something about Stone McCloud didn't add up. Granted, she didn't know many men who would be inclined to take a whole summer off to watch birds and write their names down in a little notebook. None of her friends could afford it. But even at that, he didn't add up.

For one thing, he didn't know that much about birds. Even Lucy knew piping plovers didn't nest in trees.

She suspected he was hiding something. Trouble with the IRS? Or trouble with an irate wife?

No, not a wife. She was pretty sure he wasn't married. There was that element of aloneness about him that reminded her of a stray redbone hound she'd once seen at a truck stop somewhere between Galveston and Mobile. The starving, half-wild creature had desperately wanted to come closer, but he'd been too frightened. He had leaned toward her, quivering from his eyebrows right down to his big, muddy paws, to sniff the hand she'd held out until Pawpaw had made her roll up the window. After all these years, she could still remember the half-hopeful, half-frightened look in those wary eyes.

Pawpaw had said to forget it. He'd said feral dogs knew better than to let people get too close. And Pawpaw would have known, because even with all his women and all his drinking buddies, he had been essentially a loner, too. His way of avoiding closeness was to never stay in one place too long.

Stone, a flea-bitten old road hound, and her charming, ne'er-do-well Pawpaw. Lucy had an idea that none of them would have been flattered by the comparison, and that amused her.

Her smile faded almost immediately. Stone didn't like her, and that was not so amusing. Oh, he was attracted to her—she'd seen that look in a man's eyes too many times not to recognize it. And against her better judgment, she was just as attracted to him. The sizzling current of physical awareness between them was strong enough to power the whole island, only in her case it was more than merely physical.

And therein lay the danger.

An amethyst dusk was just settling over the island when Stone came by her cottage with the picnic supper he had brought over from a deli on Hatteras. He waited outside her door, silhouetted against the pale brilliance—lean, broad shouldered, his shaggy hair still damp from a shower. Lucy forced herself not to give in to the bone-melting urge that flooded her body.

This was crazy! It was as if she hadn't learned a thing since those days when a starry-eyed teenager had lost her head, her heart and darned near lost her virginity to an Elvis look-alike with a wonderful family and the IQ of a cabbage.

"I was hoping you hadn't gotten around to eating yet," Stone said through the screen. "I ordered a take-out supper, but they loaded this thing up with enough to feed a platoon. Hard rolls with whipped horseradish butter, cold cuts, three different kinds of salad, deviled eggs. Stuff that won't hold over without risking ptomaine if the generator goes on the blink."

Lucy took control of her runaway reflexes. Common courtesy demanded that she invite him in. Simple hospitality demanded that she offer to share the dessert she had made earlier that day. It was only gingerbread from a mix, but she'd made a lemon sauce to go on top. Half-apologetically, she made the offer, and Stone let himself in, swung his basket onto the table and suggested they start with dessert.

"I haven't had gingerbread since I was a kid," he confided.

"Me, either. Too many other desserts to choose from, I guess."

They ate out on the deck. The setting was perfect for a light supper on a summer evening. The clink of silverware, of glass against glass, and the murmur of desultory conversation was accompanied by an intermittent chorus of tree frogs, the plaintive cry of a solitary chuck-will's-widow and now and then by the harsh croak of a night heron stalking the nearby shallows.

Lucy tried to maintain her guard, but it was a losing battle. She put it down to the setting. "I shouldn't have had that last glass of wine, but it tastes so good with that—what did you call it?—scallop seviche. It was sheer heaven. Did you ever wonder if angels eat? And if they do, what kind of food they eat and who cooks it? I used to wonder about that kind of thing a lot. After my mother died, Pawpaw said I used to worry about whether or not they served gumbo and cracklin' cornbread in heaven."

Chuckling, Stone refilled her glass, and she sipped and sighed. The lavender twilight gradually faded. It would be several hours before the moon rose, but the darkness was brightened by a billion or so stars, all of which were clearly visible in the absence of city lights. It reminded him of nights spent on a desert half a world away, only warmer.

And a lot more restful. The din of frogs and night birds was one thing; the sharp report of sniper fire and the roar of incoming artillery quite another.

The dangers here, he reminded himself, were more insidious, less obvious, but every bit as real. He'd do well to remember that. "You swim like a fish," he said after several minutes went by in comfortable silence. "Did you grow up on the water?"

Lucy found herself telling him about Clarence Dooley and the Dooley Trolley, about living in trailers in various oil towns and in boarding houses run by one or another of her father's lady friends. About catching crawdads and fishing for catfish and helping in the kitchen of a boarding house under the watchful eye of a landlady named Mother O'Pearl while her father worked on an offshore rig.

"Pawpaw didn't like to stay in one place too long. He always said if he'd lived in another age, he would have been an explorer."

Stone listened to Lucy's account of trying to make it to the next town on a prayer, a quarter of a tank of gas and four bald tires. Of the hair-pulling, cat-screeching fight that had taken place when one of Pawpaw's lady friends had decided to pay him a surprise visit and found him all settled in with another woman.

"I gather your father got on well with—uh, women." What else could he say? Evidently the man had had the morals of a tomcat. If that was the way he'd raised his daughter, then it was no wonder she had turned out the way she had.

"Pawpaw got on real well with just about everybody. He was so good-natured—generous to a fault. Often as not he'd give away money we didn't even have, and then we'd end up skipping out in the middle of the night when the rent came due. Unless we happened to be living with one of his lady friends, in which case, the rent money didn't seem to matter a whole lot. They all loved Pawpaw. He was a lovable man, in spite of a few minor faults."

From what she'd said, Clarence Dooley was a bum. A boozer, a brawler and a skirt chaser. Of course, his daughter wouldn't see him in quite that light, but it was easy enough for an objective party to put the pieces together and come up with an unsavory, if not all that uncommon, story. Compared to her early life, his own had been a bed of roses.

Even so, Stone couldn't condone what she had done to the Hardissons. Or what she allegedly proposed to do if she got the chance.

The next day he stopped by the Keegans' place to ask about fishing. Maudie was there alone, painting another lighthouse. There were four propped up against the walls, in varying sizes and varying colors. "Tourist art," she told him, but Stone had seen a lot worse in some pretty fancy galleries up north. "When my cataracts get bad enough," she added, laughing, "maybe I can do the kind of work that made Picasso famous."

"Don't be in too big a hurry. Personally, I like this kind of stuff, but if you're inclined to be nearsighted, you might go in for Impressionism."

"You studied art?"

"In a military school? What do you think?"

She laughed and indicated a small pile of mail on a table by the door. "Rich picked it up late yesterday, but he had to take down one of the motors to put in new bearings and he never got around to delivering it. Sorry. He's gone down to the pier again if you want bait and tackle."

Stone glanced through his mail, which consisted of two lines from the office wanting to know when he would be ready to go on assignment and a card from Reece letting him know that he could expect a houseguest in the very near future.

He was on the verge of heading down to the pier when Maudie called after him, "By the way, Mr. McCloud, I hope all our nocturnal goings and comings didn't keep you awake night before last. Rich has this weird idea that I need someone to hold my hand every time he has to leave for more than five minutes. He insisted on fetching Lucy to come sit with me while he ran over to pick up the doctor." At his frown, she went on to explain, "I had a stomach ache from eating too many fig preserves, but I'm perfectly okay now."

When he continued to look at her with growing horror, she gestured impatiently with her paintbrush and said, "I'm pregnant. It's a condition, not an illness." And then, with an impish grin, she added, "Lord knows how he'll act once I start showing."

Stone managed to make some fairly coherent response, hoping she would never learn the extent of his idiocy, and then he got out of there.

The doctor. Keegan had gone for the doctor. For his wife. He'd dragged Lucy off through the woods so she could sit with his wife until he got back. And then she had gone home.

And Stone had gone ballistic.

He had apologized for being a boor, but that didn't begin to cover the apology he owed her for being a suspicious, overbearing bastard.

In the end, he went fishing because he needed an excuse to get away by himself and think his way out of the mess he had made of everything. Granted, it was far from the first time he had made a fool of himself, but it was the first time in a lot of years that it mattered so much.

The sun was hot. What little wind there was came out of the southeast. It was heavy with moisture and hot as Hades. First he shed the life vest, then he shed his shirt, and finally his jeans, leaving him wearing his briefs and a film of insect repellent. By four o'clock in the afternoon, he had collected a headache, a stringer of panfish and a four-alarm sunburn.

Worse, he was no closer to figuring out what he was going to do about Lucy Dooley. The one thing he was certain of was that he couldn't just walk away, no matter what he discovered.

But that would come later. Before he could look after his own interests, he would have to take care of his aunt's concerns. Alice had done her duty by him; now it was time to repay the debt.

The trouble was, the more he came to know her, the more he doubted that Lucy could have ever been guilty of putting Billy though the wringer. If she'd reamed him for over half a million, where was it? She certainly didn't flash it around. And even if she had stashed away a bundle for her old age, so what? Marriage settlements were a fact of life in a lot of divorces, especially when one party was loaded and the other wasn't. That didn't mean she'd ever had any intention of tightening the screws.

Not that it would be the first time a woman had sold her self-respect by parlaying an affair with a public figure into a fortune, either directly or through book contracts, a TV series and even lecture tours. Was Lucy capable of doing that?

Alice said she was. Stone's instincts said no way!

Mooring the skiff, he returned the life vest he hadn't worn to the locker in the boathouse, put away the rod and tackle and eyed his stringer of fish with dubious pleasure. What had seemed like a good idea a few hours ago had left him no closer to a solution. Now he not only had a load of guilt and confusion to deal with, he also had a mess of fish he didn't want and third-degree burns over large portions of his body.

He stopped by the Keegans' first to offer them a fish dinner.

"Hey, don't go waving those things around where Maudie can see you. After her recent adventure, she's off fish and figs for the duration. Now she's hooked on this concoction of bananas, peanut butter and hot-chocolate mix. Stirs it all up and eats it by the bowlful. You might see if Lucy wants them. I saw her come up from the beach about a half hour ago. Hey, man, you got yourself a dose of sun!''

''Yeah, I guess I did.'' Stone had put on his clothes again. It was torture. By the time he'd made it up from the pier, he felt as if every inch of his skin had been sanded down to the bone. The last person on earth he felt like facing was Lucy, but he'd caught the damned things and it was too late now to put them back.

A few minutes later he rapped on her screened door. He could feel his pulse on the tops of his feet. That wasn't normal, was it?

She was wearing something loose and colorful that covered her from neck to ankles. Her feet were bare, brown and incongruously stubby. She looked like an overgrown angel, and in spite of his increasing discomfort, Stone felt his groin begin to stir.

''Fish?'' he asked hopefully.

''Nice. Blues and Spanish. Congratulations.''

He hadn't come there to have his ego stroked. ''You want 'em?''

''Don't you?''

''Lucy, all I want right now is to find a nice cozy snowbank and crawl in. If you don't want the things, I'm going to feel guilty as hell for catching them, and the last thing I need right now is another load of guilt.''

She held open the door, squinting against the lowering sun, and then frowned as he stepped inside. ''What on earth—? Stone, didn't you ever hear of sunscreen?''

''I make it a habit not to mix my repellents. In case you hadn't noticed, the mosquitoes are out in full force since the wind dropped.''

"That doesn't mean you can't— Well, at least you could have worn a hat and buttoned your shirt. Oh, for heaven's sake, look at your poor feet! Don't you know enough to wear socks when you go barefooted on the water in the heat of the day? Come inside and let me— Here, give me those things!"

Fussing like a broody hen, she took the fish, slung them into the kitchen sink and began fumbling around in one of the kitchen cabinets. "I've got some tea bags here somewhere...."

"If you don't mind, I won't stay for tea this time. Maybe tomorrow."

"Maybe nothing! Go wash your hands. I'm going to make you a tea ba— Ah, here they are. Quart-size ones, a full box. We're in business."

His head hadn't ached this bad in weeks. "Lucy, thanks, but I think I'd better go back to my own place. I don't feel so hot."

He might as well have been talking to a tree. She put a pot of water on to boil, dumped in an entire box of king-size tea bags and put the lid on. "Now," she said, turning back to where he stood leaning against the refrigerator, "take off your clothes. If the rest of you is in as bad shape as the parts I can see, then you're not fit to look after yourself."

Now even his stomach was beginning to rebel. He was too sick to feel embarrassed, too miserable to argue. Had he called her an angel? He'd match her up against any three small-time dictators he had run across in the course of his career.

His shoulders drooped. He felt like embracing the refrigerator just because cool steel felt better to his skin than anything he could think of at the moment.

Recognizing victory when it was within her reach, Lucy took control. It was only the fact that she was a teacher, she told herself, used to taking command in an emergency. Or maybe because she could still remember the few times in her life when she'd been sick and miserable, when someone else had taken over—when the simple fact that she didn't have to think what to do for herself had made her feel better.

It was only that, she assured herself. It certainly didn't mean she was in love with the man.

Seven

The water was lukewarm, chest deep and about the color of maple syrup. It felt better than maple syrup. In fact, it felt better than a snowbank on the Fourth of July.

Idly curious, Stone glanced around him, taking in the yellow cotton robe hanging behind the door and the almost complete lack of toiletries on the shelf beside the lavatory. Unlike the other women he had known intimately over the years, La Dooley didn't booby-trap her bathroom until a man couldn't move without knocking over half a dozen bottles or hanging himself on a pair of panty hose.

Not that he knew her intimately. At least, not as intimately as he would like to know her, he thought with wry self-honesty.

Still, it was strange, he mused as he sunk deeper in the tea bath and closed his eyes. She might have started out poor, but having married wealth, she had probably adapted pretty fast to having a maid pick up after her. He'd lay odds that right now her bedroom looked like the aftermath of a yard sale.

On the other hand...

Face it, man. La Dooley is a puzzle.

Stone had come down here expecting one thing and found another. Correction: he still hadn't figured out just what it was he had found. He hadn't expected to like her, for starters. And he did. She was damned likable. She was more than likable—she sort of grew on a guy.

By the time he had soaked in the tea bath for fifteen minutes, most of the jackhammers ripping up the inner pavement of his skull had shut down. The aspirin she'd given him must have worked, either that or her singing in the next room was more soothing than it sounded. His money was on the pills. He grinned, feeling the skin crinkle on his abused face. Actually, she had a pretty nice voice. Low, husky—easy on the ears. The trouble was, she couldn't carry a tune if her life depended on it.

Stone decided singing on key just might be a slightly overrated achievement.

"Five more minutes," she called through the door. "Keep that washcloth on your face."

Dutifully, he dipped the cloth into the bathwater again and draped it over his face, folding back one corner to make a blowhole.

"I've got a baking-soda solution for you to pat down with when you get through soaking. Close your eyes, I'm coming in."

Close his eyes?

Lucy opened the door and leaned far enough inside to set the bowl on the edge of the lavatory. "I've brought you some clothes, too, but you'd probably feel better wearing my bathrobe. It's hanging behind the door. Feel free.''

Free didn't begin to describe the way Stone felt. When he'd seen her arm and shoulder snake through the door, first with the bowl and then with a fistful of his underwear, he'd stopped breathing. And then his imagination had slipped into overdrive and he'd had to force himself to stop thinking!

He would have sworn it was physically impossible for a man in his condition to get himself into *this* condition! What he needed was a cold shower, not a warm bath.

Lucy called additional instructions through the closed door. ''You smear that soda water all over you and let it air-dry before you get dressed, you hear?''

In her own mind, the words triggered a memory of another voice, soft and fluid as New Orleans molasses, telling her to be sure to pat soda water all over her before she put on her nightgown.

Lillian had been there for her through poison ivy, cramps, childhood disease and her first broken heart, which had occurred when she'd been the only girl in her school class not invited to Violet Marie Beauchamp's birthday party. And after she'd saved up to buy her a gift!

''And wear your socks!'' she called over her shoulder as she turned back toward the kitchen. This was no time to be woolgathering, not with a pan of fillets broiling in the oven and a man soaking in her bathtub. If she didn't get her mind off the man, she was going to burn the fish.

Or was it the other way around?

Disgruntled, Stone emerged from the bathroom, looking two shades darker than a steamed hard crab, due in part to sheer embarrassment. ''Jeez, lady, didn't you get me any pants?''

"Yes, but they're not going to feel very comfortable until some of the fire goes out of those legs of yours."

"The fire's out!" he lied. "Now where the hell did you put my pants?"

"On the back of the chair." Lucy sliced a potato into a pot of water, added salt and lit the burner underneath. "Thanks to me."

One leg in, one out, Stone lifted his face to stare. She was still wearing that muumuu, or caftan, or whatever the thing was called. Did she have any idea what kind of images a tent like that gave rise to in a man's mind? And ideas weren't all it gave rise to.

"You mean, thanks to you for not throwing them on the floor?" he asked as she reached up to lift down two plates, then reached farther and opened the silverware drawer. Each movement caused the soft, colorful fabric to slide over her body like rain on a windshield. If she was wearing a single stitch underneath, it sure as hell didn't show!

"I meant, thanks to me your fire's gone out," she said calmly. "Do you want coffee, cola, water or milk to drink? We've used up all my tea bags."

Lady, if you think my fire's gone out, you'd better think again! Stone thought. Aloud, he said, "I don't suppose you have any beer?"

"No, but if you do, I'll run over and get it as soon as I—"

"Never mind, I'll get it. I'd better be getting back, anyhow. I, uh— Thanks for everything, Lucy. The bath and the soda, that is." It occurred to Stone that she hadn't once looked at him since he'd emerged from the bathroom. That wasn't like the Dooley he'd come to know. He was used to having her look him straight in the eye and give back as good as she got. He'd come to look forward to it, in fact.

Was she embarrassed at the sight of a man in his skivvies? All things considered, that was a little hard to believe. She'd had the upper hand here ever since he'd shown up on her doorstep with that damned stringer of fish.

"I padded a seat for you out on the deck, since you're in no condition to tolerate a slat-bottomed chair. Does it still hurt?"

This was getting downright embarrassing! TLC wasn't what he needed from Lucy Dooley! What he needed from her was—

"Yeah, well. It's not all that bad," he said gruffly.

"Once, when I was young, I scalded myself with boiling potlikker. A friend plastered my hand with wet tea bags and then used a baking-soda poultice, and I never even blistered. The tea and soda'll take the fire out in no time, wait and see."

It might take the fire out of his sunburn, Stone thought with reluctant amusement, but there were other kinds of fire that required an altogether different treatment. He wondered what she'd do if he asked for her help in putting out another kind of fire.

"Supper in ten minutes," she said, and he surrendered to the inevitable. The woman was one part chef, one part nurse, one part drill sergeant and ninety-seven parts temptation.

Make that ninety-seven parts trouble, he amended with a sigh.

He watched, his head beginning to throb again, while she dropped a few thin slices of onion into the potatoes, added half a can of black pepper and a blob of butter big enough to bring on cardiac arrest in a health freak.

Which he wasn't, fortunately. "Go sit!" she ordered, turning down the flame as she plopped on a lid. "I'll run over and get your beer and anything else you want."

He didn't think she was ready to hear what it was he really wanted. Sooner or later something was going to touch off an explosion between the two of them, and when it happened, they were both going to get burned. When that happened, it was going to take a lot more than tea and baking soda to put out the fire.

Some forty-five minutes later, Stone pushed away his tray, sipped on his second beer and wondered idly if he'd fried his brain along with the rest of his carcass. It wasn't like him to let anyone wait on him hand and foot this way. Especially not a woman. Especially not a woman he was supposed to be surveilling.

Or if not precisely surveilling, certainly not fraternizing with.

"Would you drink a glass of water if I poured it for you?" Lucy asked. Rising, she added his dishes to the ones on her tray and then paused beside his chair, waiting for a reply.

"Why?"

"I think you're supposed to drink plenty of fluids when you've been sunburned real bad, but I'm not sure beer qualifies."

She was standing so close, he could have leaned over a few inches and brushed his cheek against her thigh. As the thought sizzled through his consciousness, he felt his body begin to stir again—at least one of the few parts of his body that wasn't burned to a crisp.

"Why the Good Samaritan act, Lucy?" He deliberately laced the question with scepticism in an effort to throw her off-balance.

"Good Samaritan act?" She looked at him curiously. He could have sworn she was genuinely puzzled, and suddenly he felt like a dog for what he was doing to her.

Holding her gaze, he willed her to deny that it was all an act.

Willed her to prove that he was wrong about her. That Alice had been mistaken about this whole shoddy business.

He was the first to look away, but it wasn't due to guilt. At least, not entirely.

What the devil was it about those eyes of hers that made him think of bedrooms and rumpled sheets and the sweet, musky scent of sex? So they were brown. So they were big. At least half the earth's population was blessed with big brown eyes.

It had to be the combination of brown eyes and blond hair. Big, slumberous brown eyes and sun-bleached hair cropped short as a street urchin's. On a long-legged, suntanned woman with a lazy, hip-switching way of moving, the effect was damn near crippling.

Down, boy! he commanded silently. And ineffectively. He should've hung on to his tray until he had himself under better control. This was downright embarrassing!

"Hey, how about some coffee?" he suggested brightly, wishing he'd had the good sense to throw every fish he'd caught overboard before he'd come ashore.

Lucy seemed almost as relieved to escape as he was to see her go. Hearing her in the kitchen running water and clinking dishes a few minutes later, Stone wondered if she had any idea of the effect she had on men. On him in particular.

She had to have known. She was no innocent. She'd been married, and even before that she'd probably been experienced—otherwise, how had she managed to tie Billy down so fast? When it came to women, his cousin was no novice. In fact, Billy had been even more precocious with girls than he'd been with liquor, if memory served.

Lucy put the dishes in to soak while she waited for the coffee to finish dripping. By the time she went back out with the tray, she had preached herself a familiar sermon. The one that had to do with risk and involvement and pain. Silently, she vowed to drink her coffee, send McCloud on his way, hide her romances and get started on the book Frank had given her for Christmas—the one she had put off reading for nearly six months. *Lessons for Teaching in a Changing World.* In hardback, it was 634 footnoted pages!

But there were some lessons, Lucy reminded herself, that remained the same no matter how much the world changed.

"Mmm, good coffee," Stone said as he wrapped his hands around the steaming mug. He'd had time to recover and refocus. Get into it, get on with it and get out. That was the rule of thumb that had guided him safely through some of the world's most dangerous hot spots. "There's a place in Atlanta where you can blend your own and grind it to order." It was called a flank attack.

"You can do that at most supermarkets now."

"Yeah, I guess so. You been there?"

"To Atlanta? Actually, I used to live there, but I don't remember a specific coffee shop."

He waited. When she didn't elaborate, he used a few basic interrogating skills to lead her in the direction he wanted her to go, trying not to feel like a scumbag when the tactic worked. Evidently he hadn't lost his touch.

"It's not that I like big cities so much," she said in response to one of his oblique questions. "I happened to be married to an Atlantan for a while," she explained, studying her bare feet. She was sliding them slowly over the narrow cracks between the worn decking, as if she liked the feel of satiny wood against the soles of her feet.

Stone could almost feel the sensation himself, starting on the soles of his own feet, shimmering out to other parts of his body.

A soft, warm breeze blew fitfully across the island, carrying the scent of salt marsh, sun-warmed cedar, resinous pines and something more subtle—something that was uniquely Lucy. Stone steeled himself to ignore the intoxicating blend. He frowned at the shadowy, nearby woods, at the faint glow of stars showing overhead and the Pamlico Sound, gleaming like hammered silver a hundred-odd feet away.

Feeling a film of sweat break out on his back under the T-shirt, causing it to stick to his tender skin, he swore under his breath.

And then swore again at her murmur of sympathy. Dammit, he didn't want her sympathy! What he wanted was her lying naked beneath him. Or on top of him, if that was her style. Hell, he wanted her any way he could have her, but that wasn't what he'd come down here for. The sooner he could wind up this whole affair, the sooner he could start trying to patch up his self-respect!

Get on with it, man. Just do what you have to do! "You were married to Bill Hardisson, right? I thought I recognized you from somewhere. Didn't I see a picture of you and Hardisson in the *Constitution* a few years back?" There was bound to be one somewhere, sometime, he rationalized. The Hardissons were big in social, political and philanthropic circles around Atlanta, and unless he'd changed considerably, Bill never missed an opportunity to party.

Lucy closed her eyes briefly. Her hands clenched into fists in her lap, but other than that, she gave no sign of the dismay she felt. "I don't know. Yes, probably," she admitted reluctantly. She would have thought that here on Coronoke, three years and hundreds of miles away from her past, she'd have been safe.

"Well, whaddya know," Stone said thoughtfully. "So you were Bill Hardisson's wife. What do you figure his chances are in November?"

"You mean for state senator?" she replied dully. "I don't."

"You don't think he'll make it?"

"I don't think about him, period. Stone, I didn't ask— I hope caffeine doesn't keep you awake. Sleep speeds healing, you know. You'll need more than usual for the next day or so. Do you have any aspirin, by the way? I'll get the bottle for you and you can take it home with you. Take two more before you go to bed."

She was running scared. He wanted to let her get away with it, he really did. If it hadn't been for Alice, he'd have let the matter drop right there and to hell with everything.

But he'd promised. However reluctantly, he had promised his aunt to deflect any attempt she made to derail Billy's chances, and to do that he had to know what, if anything, she was up to. "Alice Hardisson—I expect she was pretty tough as a mother-in-law?"

She looked at him as if she thought it a strange observation, which it was. His usual finesse had suddenly deserted him, possibly because he was increasingly anxious to get done with the inquisition and get on with something more important. Something that had nothing to do with either his cousin or his aunt.

"Mother Hardisson was wonderful to me. I think she probably had someone else all picked out for Billy to marry, but . . ." She shrugged.

"Why do you say that?"

"She happened to be out of the country when he—when we ran off and got married, but I could see how shocked she was when she found out."

"Chopped you up into small pieces, huh?"

Lucy toyed with her coffee mug, twisting it around and around in her hands. "No, actually, she never did. In fact, she was the closest thing to a mother I've had in a long time. We got to be wonderful friends, and even now, when she doesn't have to be, she's still so good to me. I'll always be grateful for having known her."

Oh, jeez, I don't want to hear this, Stone told himself. If she'd bitched about getting the short end of the stick, torn a strip off the whole Hardisson clan, he would have felt better about what he was doing. "I've heard she can be pretty hard-nosed," he said in a halfhearted effort to steer her into a few indiscretions.

"Then you've heard wrong. Alice Hardisson is one of the kindest, most generous, most understanding women I've ever known. She had every right to be furious, but if she was, she never let on. Even though she must've been disappointed, she never let on. She was wonderful—at least, to me. I don't know if she ever said anything to Billy or not, but she never once made me feel like an outsider, and, oh, Lordy, I was a mess. I didn't know the first thing about how to dress or how to act like a lady. Mother Hardisson took me in hand and taught me everything."

"Taught you how to spend money effectively, you mean?"

She was sitting on the foot of her lounge, so close her knees were almost brushing his. "Money? Money doesn't have a blessed thing to do with being a lady." Gazing out into the darkness, she said, "Being a lady is...well, it's mostly having the kind of manners that put other people at ease. I guess it comes from being so sure of your own worth, you never have to build yourself up by cutting someone else down." She gestured helplessly with her hands. "It's a lot more than that, but I don't know how to explain it any better. All I know is that no matter what happened between Billy and me, I'll always be grateful for knowing Mother Hardisson."

Stone leaned forward. Resting his forearms on his thighs, he stared at his clasped hands, feeling like the lowest form of life, because this wasn't the way she was supposed to feel. Not about the woman who had called her white trash. The woman who called her a greedy, no-account little tramp from the Louisiana swamps, a common female with no breeding and no morals.

Suddenly he felt sick. "Look, I, uh...I think I'd better shove off. Thanks for the dinner and the bath and everything, Lucy. It helped. I feel a hundred percent better."

He felt a hundred percent worse, but it had nothing to do with having third-degree burns over a large part of his anatomy.

Stone stood up at the same instant Lucy did. They were too close. She stepped back too quickly, bumped against the edge of her chair, and Stone reached out to steady her. In the tense, overheated atmosphere, one touch was all it took. Like spark to tinder, the feel of her firm, smooth skin under his hard palm set off the conflagration he'd been trying to avoid all night.

Hadn't he?

He clasped her shoulder, cupped it and slid the thin cotton fabric against the warm skin of her back. In the faint light that spilled through the open doorway, he could see the luminous glow of her eyes, the gleam of her teeth. Her lips parted, as if she was about to speak, but she didn't. Hungrily, Stone stared down at her naked mouth. Then, with a soft oath, he lowered his head and took what she offered.

There was all the time in the world to escape, yet Lucy knew she was not even going to try. There was every reason in the world to avoid what was about to happen, but she wasn't going to avoid anything.

Except for the heartache that would come later.

The faint scent of tea surrounded his warm body. Tea, coffee, her own unscented soap and something subtly masculine and wholly intoxicating. The first touch of his mouth on hers was so gentle, she barely felt the pressure, only the heat. Touching, lifting, then touching again, his breath moist against her cheek. He kissed her a dozen times, small kisses. Devastating kisses. His hands moved down her back, slipped around her waist and then lower, pressing her tightly against his aroused body. His mouth covered hers in a fierce taking. Lucy heard him gasp. His sunburn? The pain—he shouldn't—

They *couldn't!*

Before she could react, he had deepened the kiss, and then it was too late to react to anything but the feel of him, the taste of him, the urgency of burning flesh and burning need.

His tongue explored the sensitive areas of her mouth, thrusting and withdrawing, tangling with her tongue and caressing, caressing, driving her wild with desire.

Small warnings began to sound in her brain, but were quickly drowned out by the clamor of more persistent demands.

You'll be sor-ry!

Hush! I don't want to think about it now!

This is exactly the kind of thing that always leads to trouble.

Stone would never do anything to hurt me!

He doesn't have to do anything. All he has to do is walk away.

Walk away. Which is exactly what I should be doing, Lucy told herself. Reluctantly, she turned her head aside. Stone's mouth slid lingeringly over her cheek, and then he stepped back. She wanted to wrap her arms around him again and hold on forever, but, of course, she didn't. She knew better. "Two minds with but a single thought," she whispered shakily.

"Yeah. Right." His breathing was ragged. So was hers. Was he embarrassed? Oh, Lord, don't let him be embarrassed, she thought miserably. She couldn't stand it if he was embarrassed!

"I hope I didn't hurt you, Stone—your sunburn, I mean."

He laughed, if such a raw sound could be called laughter. Turning away, he braced his hands on the railing and hunched his shoulders. Lucy ached to touch him. She half lifted her hand to his back and let it drop. There was nowhere she could touch that wouldn't be painful.

At least, nowhere she dared to touch.

The thought made her feel hot all over. Clumsily, she gathered up the coffee things and busied herself with stacking the tray before she did something irreparably stupid. Something *else* irreparably stupid, that was.

"I won't say I'm sorry, because it would be a lie," Stone said.

He was still turned away, shoulders hunched, jeans rising low on his narrow hips. They were almost as white as his T-shirt, making his skin look darker by contrast.

She'd almost fallen apart when she'd seen him ram first one leg and then the other into the faded, form-fitting denim and then suck in his flat belly to tug up the zipper. Right there in front of her, between her bathroom door and her kitchen table! She'd had the devil's own time dragging her gaze away from his crotch, and that just wasn't like her. Even in her wildest days, which weren't really all that wild, thanks to Lillian's and Ollie Mae's early warnings, she had never allowed herself to be too affected by the male physique.

Billy's had certainly never turned her blood to steam and her bones to candle wax. Under those custom-tailored suits, he was pale and doughy, with very little body hair.

Stone had body hair. On his chest and on his arms and legs, and on his face, which, this late in the day, was darkly shadowed. The tufts under his arms alone were enough to cause her knees to buckle.

Oh, Lord. "Yes," she murmured. "I mean, no—that is, it's all right. I mean, it just happened. It doesn't..."

Mean anything, she finished silently. It hadn't meant anything at all, and suddenly she knew she wanted it to mean something. She desperately wanted it to mean as much to Stone as it had to her.

* * *

Keegan's runabout brought a single passenger along with the mail the next morning. Stone was still sleeping, having lain awake for most of the night.

"Hey, guy, you in there? Hey, Stone, let me in, will you?"

Eight

Roughly a dozen years ago, Stone had fallen hard for a lovely young woman from Hamilton, Massachusetts. Shirley Stocks, daughter of a prominent surgeon, had been newly graduated from a small Virginia finishing school when they'd met. She had shyly confessed to having been engaged once before.

He had later learned from her brother, Reece, that she'd been engaged twice by the time she was nineteen, but by then Stone had been in no mood to quibble over minor details.

Shirley's had been the same kind of black-haired, purple-eyed beauty that had made Elizabeth Taylor a legend. Her looks alone had been enough to knock him off his pins, but in addition, she'd also been sweet, moderately intelligent, kind to her parents and tolerant of a younger brother who'd been something of a pain at the time. Stone's friends had all told him that he was the luckiest guy in captivity, and he'd basked in their envy.

To this day he wasn't sure exactly why it hadn't worked out, but it hadn't. Granted, they'd had little in common—still, he'd figured good sex was enough to start with. The rest would come gradually. Shirley had wanted a home and a family because that was what she'd been programmed to want. He had wanted it, too, because he'd never had it.

But evidently he hadn't wanted it enough.

Stone had been a hot-shot reporter back in those days, newly accredited, stringing for half a dozen dailies, racketing around New England in a third-hand TR-6; off at a moment's notice in search of the story that would hurtle him into the major leagues.

How many times had she made plans for them both, only to have him leave her in the lurch when he'd raced off to cover a breaking story? If it hadn't been the old woman and her umbrella capturing the red-light bandit in Newark, it was the force-five hurricane creaming the Carolinas. Or the flotilla of refugees headed for Miami, running out of food and water, with three women in labor and the Coast Guard desperately trying to reach them before they broke up in heavy seas.

There was always a story breaking somewhere. And he'd be off again, leaving Shirley to go alone to the party, or the concert, or the dance. Eventually he would return, bearing flowers, candy and abject apologies. For a few days, she would cry and he would crawl. It got to be a pattern until, after more than a year, she had handed back his ring and politely told him to drop dead. Or words to that effect.

More relieved than he cared to admit, Stone had run into her a couple of years later at the airport, wearing a diamond on her left hand that was approximately three times the size of the modest diamond he had given her. She'd been off to New York to shop for her trousseau. Having recently signed on with IPA, he'd been off on the first leg of a trip that would eventually land him in Beirut.

Reece, at that time a lanky kid of about fourteen, had tagged along with Dr. Stocks to see her off. He'd been full of questions about where Stone was going and why, about who was shooting whom and why. It had occurred to Stone at the time that he had more in common with the boy than he'd ever had with his sister. When his flight was called, Stone had kissed his ex-fiancée goodbye, offered her his best wishes and felt like a worm. When his outstretched hand had been ignored by Dr. Stocks, he'd felt a jerk.

But when he'd given Reece a high five, he had felt like a hero. The fact that they had kept in touch with each other through the years had been more Reece's doing than Stone's, although if he'd bothered to examine his feelings, Stone would have admitted that he enjoyed the infrequent contacts. Possibly because the kid reminded him of himself at that age. Too much grit for comfort, and a strong dose of idealism that was neither fashionable nor practical.

They had corresponded intermittently ever since. In one of the earlier letters, Reece had enclosed an account of his sister's wedding to a Boston investment broker. Stone had studied the grainy pictures of the stunning bride and the handsome groom and tried to convince himself that he envied the guy.

It hadn't worked. All he'd felt was guilt. Well...guilt and a little relief. Okay, guilt and a *lot* of relief.

Still, it bothered him even now when he thought about it—the fact that he was too selfish to put a woman's needs before his own ambition. The trouble was, he'd never acquired the knack of sharing himself. He'd have made her a lousy husband. In all likelihood, they wouldn't have lasted out the year. In a way, he rationalized, his ex-fiancée owed her present happiness to him. At last report, she and what's his name had three kids and were working on a fourth.

Meanwhile, Stone thought wryly, what had he accomplished in all that time?

A few awards, a certain amount of recognition, a reasonable degree of financial security and a moderate amount of satisfaction. Plus about a forty percent hearing loss in one ear and an interesting assortment of scars.

Not to mention, he added sourly, a houseguest who was currently studying journalism and seemed determined to follow in his hero's footsteps.

Stone couldn't remember when he'd felt less like a hero.

"Man, you look like hell warmed over," Reece observed cheerfully. In the few hours he had been there, he'd finished off half a bag of chips, three stale cinnamon buns, the last of the salami and a quart of milk, and was plowing through the refrigerator in search of more.

Stone sent him a disgruntled look. It was bad enough not being able to shave. Added to the itch of his fading sunburn was the itch of a three-day growth of beard. At the moment, he could do without being insulted by a human garbage disposal who looked like a cross between a star fullback and a soap opera hero. "You looking for lunch? It's barely eleven o'clock."

"I drove all night. Nothing was open."

With a reluctant grin, Stone put his own problems out of his mind. If he'd needed a distraction from this mess he'd got himself into—at least, long enough to gain some perspective—he'd found it. Unless he had changed considerably, Reece Stocks could ask more questions than Phil Donahue and the IRS put together.

On the other hand, if the questions had to do with what he was doing wasting time in a Sleepy Hollow island like Coronoke when he could be covering the latest break in the peace talks, and how long he intended to remain, he'd just as soon skip the whole business.

"If you're still hungry, step aside," Stone growled. "Actually, you're in luck. I do a great sardine and sauerkraut sandwich, with or without onions."

"You're serious, aren't you?"

"You wanna eat, or don't you? This place isn't like home, you know. You can't just call in an order to the nearest takeout."

Reece wasn't critical. Food was food. Over a meal consisting of whatever they could scrounge from Stone's few remaining supplies, they discussed Reece's current studies, the Balkan situation and the political agenda of several of his teachers.

Stone, feeling avuncular and just a little bit sad at this living reminder of the swift passage of time, spoke of the dangers of going into a story with a preconceived idea. They argued about whether a lack of prejudice was possible in this age of instant information.

Warming to the subject, they argued the differences between objectivity, subjectivity, personal opinion and political bias. Nothing was solved, but by the time they'd cleaned out his cupboards and polished off his last six-pack and a pint of grapefruit juice, Stone was feeling considerably better about life in general. His feeling of well-being lasted until Reece sat up, gave a long, low whistle and said, "Hey, I think I'll check out the beach. See you later, okay?"

Stone knew exactly what it was his guest was planning on checking out. It had nothing to do with the local landscape. "Yeah, sure," he muttered. "You don't mind if I don't tag along?"

"Hey, man, you need to take care of that burn! I'd stay out of the sun for the rest of the week, if I were you."

Sure you would, Stone thought with bitter amusement. "Follow the path until you come to a big dead cedar out on the edge of the water. Look to your right and you'll see some markers a couple hundred feet offshore. It's clear of obstacles all the way out and deep enough for some decent swimming."

Although he seriously doubted that doing laps was what Reece had in mind.

From the deck, Stone watched the boy jog down the sandy path, a towel around his eighteen-inch neck and a few square inches of purple spandex swaddling his crotch. Leaning back, he closed his eyes and tried to force himself to sleep, but in spite of the fact that he was physically tired, the wheels refused to stop turning. He'd tossed and turned in bed until his skin was so sore he had finally gotten up and come out onto the deck, where he'd stayed until daylight, watching the cottage next door. Thinking about the woman sleeping inside, her long legs sprawled in inviting abandon. Wondering what he was doing down here in the first place, and what the hell he was going to do about her.

He knew what he'd like to do.

Lucy waded out until the water came up to her hips, then dived under and swam until she ran out of air. She swam laps until her arms and legs felt like lead, until her strokes began to lose their power and her kicks barely fluttered the water.

It wasn't working. She could swim to Bermuda and back and it wasn't going to do one blessed thing for her state of mind.

Well, friend, you've really done it now, she told herself. After all my lectures about the dangers of wanting things you can't have, of creating an image in your mind and mistaking it for reality, you've gone and done it again, haven't you? For a woman who worked so hard to get an education, you sure didn't learn very much.

"Hey, how's the water?"

She missed a stroke, felt her feet begin to sink and churned water with her arms to compensate. Blinking the salt from her eyes, she stared at the silhouette of the man splashing toward her, and her heart started knocking against the walls of her chest.

And then it settled down again. Whoever he was, he wasn't Stone. And if he wasn't Stone, then she didn't care who he was. And if that didn't add up to disaster, she didn't know what did.

He was young, she saw when he came within range, and extremely good-looking. A real hunk, in fact—the kind of boy her older girls gigglingly referred to as *so-o-o fine!*

"Five laps between markers is about a mile. I think."

"I figured it was about that," said Reece, who hadn't even noticed the markers, he'd been so busy admiring the front view of what he'd only seen a side and a back view of from Stone's deck.

From the front, she was even more terrific. A little older than he'd expected, but then, he'd always subscribed to the theory that the best women, like the best wine, improved with age.

They got through the preliminaries, and when Lucy pleaded exhaustion and headed toward shore, Reece turned and slogged along beside her, friendly as a spaniel.

Who could help responding? He made no effort to hide his admiration, but neither did he make an issue of it. He was, in a word, friendly. And right now, Lucy told herself, she could use a friend, even a temporary one who was probably ten years her junior.

"Which cottage is yours?" he asked, and she told him. If he began to make a pest of himself, she could always hook the screen door. In a place like Coronoke, that would be enough. Like taking in the welcome mat.

"I'm staying with Stone McCloud—you probably met him already. He's a friend from way back. In fact, he's the real reason I'm studying journalism."

Lucy didn't want to talk about Stone. She didn't want to think about him. He had told her what he did for a living when she'd pressed him, and then waited expectantly. She hadn't known what he expected, so she'd said something about not really thinking he made a living with his bird-watching, and after a while they'd gone on to talk about something else.

"Where are you from?" she asked Reece. He was vigorously drying his dark blond hair, flexing his muscles just a bit more than necessary, she suspected.

"Massachussetts. How about you?"

"Here and there." She didn't want to talk about herself. She didn't want to talk at all, but it was better than brooding. As long as he kept talking, she didn't have to think. Hoping to prime the pump, she asked if he had any brothers or sisters.

Which led them right back where they started.

"My sister, Shirley—she was how I met Stone in the first place. I was just a kid then. Shirl's a lot older than me. She was engaged to Stone once—my sister was always getting engaged. Like, she played with dolls from the time she was born, and she had this dollhouse and all? And she used to threaten to carve out my liver if I ever laid a hand on it. All she used to talk about was how she was going to have her own house with a maid and all, so she could concentrate on being a wife and mother. I mean, can you believe any girl these days would be dumb enough to admit it, even if she felt like that?"

Lucy laughed dutifully. Yes, she could believe it. Career feminists notwithstanding, some women were born with a stronger nesting instinct than others. Hadn't she dragged around from Louisiana to Texas, from Texas to Georgia, and from Georgia to North Carolina, the same old leggy houseplants, the same old framed snapshots, the same ratty wicker basket her father used to drop his socks and shirts in to be mended by whichever woman happened to be keeping him at the time, and the same old shabby guitar case that always stood in the corner of whatever place they'd called home?

Lucy had been liberated a long time ago. She stood on her own two feet, supported herself and asked nothing from anyone. She built her own nests, the way she always had.

But she could sympathize with a woman who dreamed of making a home—of making babies—with a certain lean, gray-eyed, dark-haired man whose frown could make the sun disappear and whose smile could make the stars shine twice as bright.

She wanted to know which of them had broken the engagement, and because she wanted it so badly, she didn't ask. Reece mentioned the Heels' chances of getting a bowl bid next year after losing their three most valuable players in one season. Fortunately, he didn't seem to notice that her responses were less than informed, and even less interested. He talked sports while she drowsed.

He was a sweet boy, she mused, lying on her stomach while the late-afternoon sun baked into her bones. A nice, undemanding companion. Maybe a dose of undemanding companionship was just what the doctor ordered. Solitude left too much time to think.

"Wanna have a wiener roast tonight? We could run over and get supplies. Stone's fresh out of food, and being around all this water gives me an appetite, whaddya say? You game?"

Stone was waiting at her place when she got back. His burn had faded in spots, giving him a patchy look that should have been unattractive, yet somehow managed to make him even more appealing.

Or maybe there was just something inherently appealing about any sign of vulnerability in an otherwise invulnerable man.

"You look as if you've been enjoying life," he observed when she waved away the mosquitoes, stepped inside the screened deck and slung her sandy towel over a chair back.

"You look as if you're enjoying it now," she retorted.

He didn't. He might have faded, he might be sprawled out in her most comfortable lounge chair, but there was something about him—in the set of his shoulders, the arms crossed over his chest and the hard glint in his cool eyes—that said otherwise.

"I take it you met my houseguest?"

"Reece? Yes, I did."

Was it her imagination, or was there something challenging in the highly charged atmosphere? After a long, drowsy afternoon following an exhausting hour of swimming laps, Lucy was in no mood to be challenged. Not by anyone, not for any reason.

"Was there something you wanted?" she asked pointedly. "I'm meeting Reece on the pier as soon as I shower and change, so—"

"He's a little young for you, isn't he?"

She lifted her eyebrows. "Is he? So maybe I'll adopt him."

"He's already got two functioning parents."

"And a sister, I understand. Shirley?"

"What has he been telling you about— No, forget it. Just forget it, okay?" Stone levered himself up from the wood-slat chair. Every crack and every plank was embossed on his tender backside, but that was the least of his worries.

"I already have."

He was standing in front of her door, and as he didn't seem inclined to move out of her way, she was forced to brush past him to get inside.

"Lucy?" He was so close, she could smell his soap and the slight minty scent of toothpaste. He wore the same old faded jeans and the same old limp khaki shirt. "Could we talk?"

"I don't think so, Stone. I told you, I'm meeting—"

"Yeah, right. You're meeting Reece for a moonlight sail. The moon won't be rising for another eight hours, minimum, so spare me a few minutes, will you?"

From the smooth look of his angular jaw, he'd recently shaved. She could see the marks of a comb through his still-damp hair. He was shower-fresh, and she was beach-grungy. Salty, sticky and sandy.

"Stone, I really don't think we have anything to talk about."

She edged past, but he reached out and touched her cheek in a slow, deliberate caress. When his hand fell to her shoulder, her stricken gaze flew to his. "Please," she whispered. "Don't do this to me."

"Then don't be so damned stubborn." His other hand reached out to bar the door, and he pulled her, unresisting, toward him. Heat instantly flared around them. Lucy caught her breath, powerless to resist what she so desperately needed.

"Stone, I don't know what it is you want from me."

"Yes, you do," he muttered. His hands moved on her waist, his fingertips meeting at her spine and then sliding forward again to shape the bones of her hips. "You know damned well what I want, lady, because you want it just as much as I do. And I want it so much, I can taste it."

"But we don't even particularly like each other," she lied. "It doesn't make sense!"

"Tell me about it," he groaned, pulling her head down onto his shoulder. Her damp, sandy bathing suit was pressed tightly against his dry, hot body. The scent of laundry detergent, toilet soap and the clean, musky essence of healthy female flesh drifted up on waves of heat, the effect irresistibly intoxicating.

He was angry and aroused. His arousal aroused her and his anger heightened the effect. Lucy didn't know why he was angry, but it didn't seem to matter. Nothing mattered at that moment but the fierce urgency that drew them together like steel to a magnet.

"You're driving me crazy," he said hoarsely, burying his face in the curve of her throat. "I can't sleep for thinking about what it would be like to lay you down and—"

"Don't!" she pleaded. "Don't say it!"

His tongue traced small circles on her salty skin. "I don't have to say it. You're thinking the same thing I'm thinking."

"No, I'm not!"

Step by step, he backed her into the living room, his arms supporting her, his lean, muscular thighs sliding against hers in a way that drove her wild. "How do you know you're not, if you're not thinking the same thing I am?" he purred, his mouth moving over her temple, down her cheek, following the curve of her jaw.

Just inside the door, his teeth closed over the tip of her chin, and she gasped. Before she could turn away, he captured her lips, and then it was too late.

"The screen's not even hooked," she murmured a long time later, and then stood there like a stump while he went back to hook it.

"Now it is," he said, picking up where he'd left off.

Eventually they made it as far as her bedroom, if not quite as far as the bed. Stone leaned against the edge of the dresser, his legs spread, while he slowly peeled the straps of her faded blue tank suit down over her shoulders.

Pressed against the swollen fork of his thighs, Lucy could feel his heat, his eagerness, and it inflamed her to the point where, trembling, she could hardly stand.

"We're going to regret this," she said in one last effort to bring sanity into an insane situation.

"Not as much as we'd regret missing it."

"Stone, this is all wrong! What if—"

"Kindly shut up, love," Stone muttered, his mouth covering hers with a demand she was only too eager to meet.

Rocking his mouth over hers, Stone willed himself not to rush her. He had fantasized about this since the first moment he'd laid eyes on her. Right or wrong didn't enter the picture, nor did regrets. Those he would handle when he had to. Right now, all he could think of was taking her, making love to her until neither of them could think straight, and then doing it again and again.

Maybe then he could make sense of whatever it was between them. Because something sure as hell was. He only hoped it was purely physical, because he wasn't cut out for anything more than that.

Her lips were like cool satin, the inside of her mouth more like hot satin. He devoured her, drowning in the flavors—the salt, the sweet, the essence that was hers alone. Totally without artifice, she was more intoxicating than any woman he had ever known, much less made love to.

She unbuttoned his shirt and unsnapped the top of his jeans. "Ah, sweetheart, don't touch me there. It's been a long time," he groaned.

Lucy tried to force herself to move her hands back up the flat expanse between his belt and the thatch of hair on his chest. She traced the irregular line of a pale pink scar low on his belly and wondered about it briefly, before she was too distracted even to think.

He was delicious all over, and she was drunk with desire. Never before in her life had she felt this way—never this wild, driven hunger to touch, to taste, to experience a man with all her senses, to become a part of him, physically, emotionally—and more.

He buried his face between her breasts, cupping them together with his hands while his thumbs circled the tightly furled buds at their tips. She shuddered, her thighs tensing and dissolving until she thought she would collapse where she still stood, in the circle of his arms.

"We've got to move to the bed," she gasped. "My bones have all melted."

"Mine, too—all except one." His shaky laugh rippled down her sensitive nerves like fingertips over the strings of a harp.

Somewhere between the dresser and the bed, Stone managed to shed the rest of his clothes. As Lucy's suit was hanging around her hips, she shoved it down and stepped out of it. Bits of gravel stuck to her legs and a few to her buttocks, but she was beyond caring.

Stone knew his legs wouldn't support him much longer, but for one long moment he was incapable of moving. He stood and stared at the woman sprawled across the bed. She was everything he had imagined and more. The areas of her body that were untouched by sun only served to emphasize her small brown nipples and the narrow golden pelt that rose high on her flat belly.

She was magnificent. She was incredible. She was... Lucy.

"Stone, where did you get that?" she inquired a moment later, touching the three small, round scars high up on the outside of his left thigh.

"About five hundred kilometers south of Baghdad."

"And that one?" She touched the scar on his belly.

"Somalia."

"When you said you were a journalist, I never expected— That is, I thought— What about this one?"

When he'd rolled over to hide the bullet holes that puckered his thigh, she had discovered the thin line that ran along his lower spine. He didn't want to talk about his scars. He didn't want to talk about what it was he did. He didn't want to talk about the fact that for years he had roamed the globe, afraid of settling in any one place, rejecting the possibility of putting down roots because roots could be ripped up in an instant, and those wounds could be devastating.

He didn't want to talk about any of that, because he had never told any woman how he felt deep down inside where he lived.

He didn't want to talk at all.

Neither did Lucy. Aching from suppressed need, she wanted to experience everything at once. Only, then it would be over. After today or tomorrow—after a week or perhaps a month—he would be gone and so would she.

Would she be sorry? Probably.

Would that prevent her from taking what he was offering her now? Not in a million years!

They came together explosively that first time. All it took was one more searing, searching, thrusting kiss— one more touch of Stone's hand sliding down the slope of her belly, and her own hand moving toward the heat of his hard desire.

With a muffled exclamation, he reached for his jeans, ripped open the flat foil pack, and a moment later, pushed her over onto her back to move between her thighs. "I warned you about playing with fire," he grated.

Her hips rose eagerly to meet him. Eyes clinging to his, she whispered, "I've never been good at taking advice . . . it's my only failing."

There was no holding back. He came into her, and she wrapped her long legs around his waist and bit her lip, her face flushed with passion.

"Beautiful—too beautiful— I can't—"

It was over too quickly, yet neither of them would have had it otherwise. Stone collapsed, with a quiet sense of fulfillment. Lucy bore his full weight cradled against her until he rolled aside.

Later, he took her again. This time, he lifted her on top of him, savoring her golden beauty, her strength, the honesty that shone from her glowing face.

Honesty. His mind tried instinctively to reject the thought, only to have it cling there, like a pesky sandbur.

Strength, honesty, a basic innocence and an utter lack of malice. This was the real Lucy, no matter what—

But then she began to move, and there was no more room for thought, no room for doubts—no room for anything except this wild, incredible pleasure that made rational thought impossible. Hands on her hips, he guided her, their movements increasingly frantic. The ragged sounds of their breathing tore through the late-afternoon silence, accompanied by broken words, small cries and then a long, shaken groan.

This time it was Lucy's turn to collapse, Stone's turn to hold her. The smell of sex and clean linens was all around them. A light breeze came through the open window, cooling their damp bodies. Lightly, his hands stroked her smooth back, and then he tenderly slid his palms over the curve of her buttocks, savoring the firmness of her healthy flesh.

God, she was magnificent! Even half dead, he wanted her again!

Stone was no stranger to women, although he had always been highly selective. But Lucy was in a class by herself. He had never experienced anything even faintly like this. There were no words to describe the difference, nor did he try. But it was there, all the same. And that made him uneasy, because now that his mind was beginning to function again, he was starting to suspect the difference might not be entirely physical.

Damn. As if things hadn't been awkward enough before! This could change everything. All his survival instincts told him that this particular situation was going to take some careful handling not to blow up in his face.

For a long time he simply watched her. It was a surprisingly pleasant thing to do. She slept like a child. No—more like a cat. Limp. Boneless. She even purred like a cat, a quiet little humming sound that came from somewhere in her throat.

Stone found himself wondering about her marriage—about what she had seen in his cousin. It was pretty clear what Billy had seen in her. The same thing any man would see.

Any man, including Reece, he thought, cursing quietly as someone banged on the hooked screen door.

"Hey, Lucy! You in there?" A pause, and then, "Anybody home?" The door rattled against the frame. "Stone? Is Lucy in there?"

Nine

Analytical skills honed by years of practice clicked into action. Stone didn't hurry the process, despite the fact that Lucy was lying beside him in bed and Reece was only a few feet away, pounding on the front door. The problem was that there was no way he could pretend to be an objective observer—not this time. This time he'd screwed up big time. This time he had dived in headfirst without bothering to check the depth. This time he had acted impulsively, and J. Stone McCloud, accredited IPA journalist, widely experienced and modestly acclaimed, with a recent flattering offer to syndicate a weekly column, didn't have an impulsive bone in his body. Either personally or professionally.

So the question was, why had he done it?

The answer came back immediately: how the hell did *he* know why he'd done it? He'd wanted her and she was available, right?

"Wrong," he muttered under his breath. There was more to it than that. These days, no man with a functioning brain dared act so irresponsibly. And while admittedly his brain hadn't been functioning up to peak standards just lately, he could have sworn it hadn't shut down completely until right there at the end.

Reece called out again, and Stone scowled, picturing the big, good-looking kid with muscles bulging out of his sleeveless shirt and a grin that could bring on a core meltdown in any female under the age of eighty.

And then the truth slammed into him like a runaway tank.

Stone whispered an obscenity. He'd thought he was smart? Prided himself on being the kind of guy who could walk into any scene cold and, using only his eyes and his incisive intellect, quickly winnow fact from chaff? Hell, he wasn't fit to cover a cookie bake-off at a county fair!

Lucy stirred beside him. Sighing, she wriggled her bottom snugly into the curve of his body, and against all reason, his groin began to stir again. Stone swore. Reluctantly he moved away, sat up and lowered his feet to the gritty floor.

Okay, so now that he knew what had happened, what was he going to do about it?

Hell, they both knew what had happened. He'd finally even figured out why, and the knowledge was neither flattering nor comfortable. What he'd done was to stake his claim. Put his brand on her. Primitively stated, he had marked his territory. He had come down here with a clear-cut objective and ended up behaving in a way that was not only unprofessional, it was damned near unforgivable!

His lips twisted in a bitter parody of humor. All it had taken was seeing her with another man—a younger, stronger man—and he'd come charging in like a wild stallion to protect his favorite mare.

His? That was a joke. At the moment, however, Stone didn't feel much like laughing. Lucy stirred and rolled over onto her back so that she was no longer touching him. Feeling the loss, he started to reach out and draw her back, catching himself just in time.

And that was scary, too.

"Hi, there," she said huskily, her eyes still closed. "Guess I fell asleep, huh?"

Against his better judgment, Stone leaned over and braced his weight on one arm. His smile was a little twisted, and it never quite reached his eyes. "I guess we both did."

Blinking at the late-afternoon sunlight slanting through the window, Lucy gazed up at him. For one brief instant he thought he saw something in her glowing face that knocked the wind right out of his sails, but then the front screen rattled again, and Reece yelled out something about supper on the beach, and Stone decided that what he'd seen had been confusion. Or embarrassment.

Or maybe speculation, he told himself, knowing damn well he was only trying to cover his own tail. "Shall I get rid of him?"

"No, I—I promised." She began to edge away, and Stone forced himself to back off. He needed more time and space to get a handle on what had hit him. Taking a woman to bed was nothing out of the ordinary, but feeling like a bombed-out cathedral afterwards most definitely was.

Perspective. That was what he lacked. However, perspective would have to wait, because at the moment, there was an impatient young stud on her doorstep who sounded as if he might just remove the door from its hinges and see for himself what was going down.

"I'd better go." Lucy rolled out of bed and reached lethargically for her caftan.

"I'll go. Take your time." Stone stepped into his jeans, dragged on his shirt and raked his fingers through his hair. Trying not to look as if he'd just climbed out of bed, he sauntered through the house to unhook the screen door.

"Stone? What's going on? Isn't this Lucy's place?"

"She's in the—uh, bathroom. Sorry about the door. I must've hooked it out of habit when I came over to, uh—borrow a book." *Smooth, man—real Academy Award stuff.*

"Sure. No problem, just a few raw knuckles." Reece was obviously burning with curiosity, but he had sense enough not to push it. He pretended an interest in the deck furnishings, which were practically identical to those on Stone's deck.

Stone flexed his shoulders. Reluctantly, he stepped away from the doorway, allowing Reece inside the living room. "Lucy'll be out in a minute. She had to...uh..."

"Hey, man, it's cool." He glanced around the room, looking somewhat uncomfortable, and then turned to face Stone. Taking a deep breath, he said, "Look, if I'm in the way, just say so and I'll back off, no sweat. If you two have something going for you..."

"The lady makes her own decisions. Ask her."

"I already did. At least, I asked her if she wanted to cook out on the beach tonight. I thought it was all set, but maybe—"

"Then it's all set," Stone said with a shrug. Which is my cue to leave, he told himself. He'd made his feelings known, hadn't he? The next move was hers.

Still, he stood his ground while Reece prowled. Picking up a thick book with a drab dustcover from the coffee table, the younger man glanced at the title and then dropped it onto a stack of paperbacks, scattering them across the polished surface. Next he moved over to the corner to open the guitar case that stood there. He ran a thumb discordantly across the strings, then, closing the case, he let it fall back carelessly against the wall.

Stone moved quickly to right the case before it slid to the floor. With a tightly leashed energy that was totally out of character, he strode across the room to the coffee table and neatly restacked her books. It occurred to him that he was being territorial again, and he didn't bother to deny it, chalking it up to the residual effects of six weeks in the hospital, plus an overdose of sun.

Yeah. Sure. Or maybe the hole in the ozone layer.

Reece was watching him curiously. Finally he shrugged and said, "Hey, look, I guess you can join us if you want to. I meant to take her over to Hatteras, pick up some beer and wieners and then come back and spend the night on the beach, watching the stars and stuff, but I guess I owe you a meal, at least."

"At the very least," Stone said grimly, forced to acknowledge a streak of meanness he would have preferred to deny. But when he saw the way Reece's face fell at the thought of a cozy threesome, he relented. "On second thought, I could do with an early night. You kids have a ball."

Reece didn't even bother to hide his relief.

Kids, hell, Stone thought a few minutes later as he stalked across the shadow-streaked sand to his own place.

Reece might not be old enough to know any better, but Lucy sure as hell was!

From his own deck a little while later, Stone heard an outboard sputter a couple of times and roar off. He listened until the sound faded, then congratulated himself on being generous and open-minded.

Like hell. He felt mean, selfish and vindictive.

For the first time since he'd arrived, he dug out his Walkman and put on a Redpath tape. Bad choice. Instead of cheering him up, the music only stirred up long-dead ashes of an old dream. The last thing he needed tonight was a bunch of sad songs about old men, abandoned homes and the kind of gut-wrenching loneliness that could catch a guy off-balance and knock him for a loop.

Abruptly, Stone snapped off the tape player and wished he had something stronger than beer on hand, because there came a time in a man's life when he needed something to take the edge off.

He had logic on his side. It wasn't doing the job.

Dammit, they'd had sex! It wasn't as if they'd even pretended it was anything more! It had been good, sure—hell, it had been terrific—but it was only sex. No more, no less.

Later, he watched the glow of a bonfire on the beach and thought longingly of the ritual rain dances of various cultures he had run across in his career. Unfortunately, there wasn't a hint of a cloud to dim the brilliance of a million-odd stars. Stalking into the kitchen, he drank half a quart of milk and went to bed. If they stayed out there all night, he didn't want to know about it.

Unfortunately, the silent battle refused to end there.

She wouldn't, he told himself sometime after midnight. Not after today. Even if she'd been the slut Alice had described—and he knew in his heart she wasn't—Lucy wouldn't do that, because she'd know that Stone would know, and she had more class than that.

Besides, Reece was just a kid.

Dammit, Reece was no kid, he was a man! If even half the stuff he bragged about in his letters was true, then he was a damned stud! Stone's own college days were long behind him, but unless he'd forgotten his basic biology, men and women reached their respective sexual primes at different ages.

Sexually speaking, both Reece and Lucy were at the prime of life, while if the experts could be believed, Stone was on the downhill slope, his prowess on the decline.

A modest decline, granted, if today's performance was anything to judge by, but still...

"Ah, damn!" he muttered, and rolled over onto his back to stare up at the slowly revolving blades of the ceiling fan overhead.

Lucy tried to tell herself that nothing had changed, that she and Stone had simply succumbed to a moment of weakness. It had been no more than that—a moment of weakness. They were both of age. Neither of them was married, and as far as she knew, neither of them had any other attachment. They were entitled.

Naturally one had to be careful, but these days, sex was considered just another appetite. Like chocolate. Or a craving for collard greens and corn dumplin's. As far back as she could remember, her own father had gone from woman to woman like a bee in a flower garden, and no one had thought any less of him for that.

Of course, Lillian had always bristled whenever Ollie Mae's name was mentioned, and Ollie Mae swore that Lillian's red hair came from a bottle, although the two women had never met. As for poor Coralee down in Mobile, she'd been jealous of every other woman in Clarence Dooley's life, but then, Coralee hadn't lasted long. Pawpaw had always said a body had to bend with the wind or break, and he had chosen to bend. Actually, he had bent just about every rule in the book, yet he'd been happier than any man Lucy had ever known, before or since.

The one time Lucy had stood against the wind, holding out for a wedding ring, a home and the prospect of children who wouldn't be reared like Gypsies, she had come perilously close to breaking.

Which just went to prove something or other, she told herself, only she wasn't sure it was going to do her much good.

The Keegans invited the island's handful of residents to a smoked-fish supper on Sunday evening. A couple from Fort Wayne were scheduled for the Seymore Cottage, Blackbeard's Hole, and a family of five would be renting The Whistling Swan.

Lucy was glad of the distraction. Reece was fun to be with, but a little of him went a long way. She was afraid that he was developing a crush on her. That sort of thing happened fairly often, and as a rule she handled it with a mixture of tact and firmness that didn't ruffle any feathers and left everyone's pride intact, but at the moment she wished she didn't have to make the effort. She had a lot on her mind.

Stone was avoiding her. The day after *it* had happened, she had avoided him, too, needing time to think.

She had left early to spend the day over on Hatteras and ended up doing the shops, visiting the museums, getting her hair trimmed and watching the windsurfers at Canadian Hole.

The haircut had been a spur-of-the-moment decision. Reece met her on the path to the pier and invited himself along, and she'd put him off with the flimsy excuse of having to get her hair done, which meant she had to find someone who could take her without an appointment because she wasn't comfortable with the lie.

She'd learned later that he and Stone had gone fishing.

The next day, Stone went fishing alone. From the swimming area, Lucy had seen him anchored a few hundred yards off the tip of the island at the edge of the channel. He was wearing a hat, she was glad to note—an Australian bush hat that looked as if it might have been trampled by a herd of kangaroos. He wore a shirt, too, and as far as she could tell, it was buttoned up the front. At least she wouldn't have to worry about his getting blistered again—he'd learned his lesson. In fact, he was beginning to build up a nice protective coat of tan.

And, anyway, she told herself, it was none of her business if he went out stark naked in the heat of the day and burned to a crisp.

But inside her, a small, persistent ache began to deepen. Reasonable or not, she couldn't seem to help caring. He wasn't hers to care about and he never would be. And knowing it, she still cared. So much for learning from her mistakes.

"Hey, wanna go for a dip before we head on over to the Keegans'?" Reece asked. It was Sunday, and he'd evidently been jogging around the perimeter of the island, wearing only a pair of the brief cutoffs he seemed to favor and a towel around his neck. He was barely panting, the film of sweat on his handsome face only adding to his clean-cut good looks.

Lucy had been idly drawing pictures in the sand with a stick, her mind a million miles away. Or rather, a few hundred yards away. "I promised Maudie I'd do a salad, and I haven't even started yet."

"Plenty of time. Stone's still out fishing. Been out there every day lately. You'd think he'd get bored after a while."

"Is he planning to come to the cookout?"

Reece shrugged his massive shoulders. "Beats me. It's a free meal, but he's never been big on socializing."

"You've known him a long time?"

"Oh, sure. Like I told you, Stone was supposed to be my brother-in-law, only he got cold feet. I guess he's always been a loner. Probably why he's so good at what he does—he never lets anything derail that one-track mind of his."

Lucy made an attempt to revive her sagging spirits. So what else was new? She'd had him pegged for a loner all along. Reece had only corroborated what she'd already known.

"Man, I've been smelling that grill of Keegan's all day! If I don't get something to eat pretty soon, I'm going to cave in!"

"Is that all you think about—food?"

"Hey, lady, I'm a growing boy, in case you haven't noticed!"

She laughed, falling in beside him. There was a new degree of ease between them that told her he had gotten her message. "Believe me, I've noticed! Tell your mama the next time you see her that her little boy's outgrowing all his clothes.'' She eyed his skimpy attire.

He favored her with an engaging grin, one she suspected had melted more than one young female heart. "You noticed, huh? Hey, Luce—you know what just occurred to me? What this place needs is a supermarket. And maybe a take-out place.''

"Are you planning to move in and start up an industry? I thought you were studying to be a journalist.''

"Well, I am. I just hate to see a great opportunity go to waste, that's all.''

"Forget it. It would never work. There's hardly enough room, and besides, it would spoil the atmosphere.''

"Can't eat atmosphere,'' he quipped. Flicking her on the rear with his towel, he said, "Go do your salad while I change into my dinner jacket, and I'll walk you over to the Keegans'.''

Stone came late. Lucy was serving plates while Maudie shuttled between the grill where Rich Keegan presided and the makeshift table that had been set up on the largest porch. The wind had picked up to blow the mosquitoes away, and the hum of desultory conversation rose and fell against the perennial background sound of lapping water. Overhead, the sky was a deep, clear gray, with molten streaks of color layering the western horizon. Venus pulsated above the silhouetted trees.

Lucy had just served the last of the smoked fillets and was waiting for the platter to be refilled when Stone stepped up onto the porch. Her gaze locked unerringly with his, and for a small eternity they stared at one another. It couldn't have been more than a few seconds at the very most, yet during that time she felt her heartbeat accelerate like a runaway train. Sweat beaded her skin, and she dropped the serving fork with a clatter.

She had only imagined that look, she told herself a few moments later as she lifted a fillet of grilled Spanish mackerel onto a plate and added a serving of roasted potatoes. Still, she followed his progress as he made his way to where the men were gathered on the other side of the porch.

Maudie came with another platter of grilled tuna. Reece waved Stone into the group and called on him to settle a question about some political scandal or other, and Lucy went on serving, putting smaller portions on the children's plates and answering the eager questions about the frosted cake on the makeshift buffet.

"Don't you dare tell 'em it's carrot cake. Mine won't touch anything that even sounds like a vegetable," said Micki Branscomb.

"Don't tell me beta-carotene can survive forty-five minutes at three-fifty degrees," Maudie scoffed. She dropped down into a chair and rested her palms protectively on her still-flat stomach.

"Who cares? It's my conscience I'm worried about. Do they look like they're starving to you? If they get any more energetic, I'm going to use them to recharge batteries. I swear I am!"

They all laughed: Lucy; Micki, a thirtyish legal secretary and mother of three; Maudie, at forty, newly married, newly pregnant and the owner of a rambling ruin that was perennially in the throes of renovation; and Cassie Miranda, a grandmother whose wedding rings had probably cost as much as Lucy earned in a year.

Lucy had always enjoyed the company of women. Thanks to Alice, she felt perfectly comfortable with women of all ages and levels of society. While the men discussed politics and sports on one side of the room, the women discussed work and books on the other. Once it was learned that Lucy was a schoolteacher, the talk turned to children. And when Maudie revealed her pregnancy, they switched over to a discussion of childbirth, weight gains, prenatal care and postnatal blues.

Lucy excused herself and slipped inside to use the bathroom. Anything she might have added to the conversation would only have made the others uncomfortable. She never talked about her own pregnancy. Sometimes she was able to go for weeks without even thinking about it, but a part of her would always wonder. A part of her would always ache for what was irretrievably lost.

Unwilling to return just yet, she lingered inside, absently examining the Keegans' extensive collection of books. Some were new, some obviously old, the titles barely legible against the aged leather bindings. Was that *Owl* something-or-other and *Isdom at the War, Vol. III?*

A closer examination revealed the full title: *Knowledge and Wisdom of the World, Vol. III.*

"Oh, great," she muttered. "Just my luck." Now that it was too late to do her any good, she had finally discovered a source of knowledge and wisdom. "Where were you when I needed you?"

She was still holding the book in her hand when Stone joined her a few minutes later. "Are you all right?" he asked.

Carefully, Lucy replaced the book on the shelf. "I'm fine, and you? No more sunburn, I'm glad to see. Did you catch any fish today?" His clear gray eyes searched her own, and she could have kicked herself for letting him know that she'd been watching him. "Reece mentioned you'd gone fishing."

"No fish, no burn. I fell asleep and forgot to rebait my hook."

He was standing just a tiny bit too close, deliberately invading her personal space. Lucy suspected it was deliberate, because Stone seldom did anything without a purpose. He wasn't an impulsive type.

"I haven't seen much of you in the past couple of days," he said.

"I've been busy."

"So I noticed."

The air in the spacious room suddenly became charged. It was warm, humid—a typical late June evening—yet Lucy felt chill bumps forming on her body. "Did you, uh— The grilled fish was good, wasn't it? Did you know Rich was an officer in the air force? He's from this small town in—"

"Lucy, I don't give a sweet damn where Keegan's from, and neither do you. Are you all right?"

The color fled from her face, leaving her looking older than her years, yet oddly vulnerable. "Are you asking if I'm pregnant? For goodness' sake, Stone, it's only been a few days."

"I know how long it's been, dammit! I also know there's a certain time of the month when conception is possible, and we didn't use anything the last two times. What I want to know is, is it possible for you? Are you taking anything?"

Anger blazed in her eyes as the heat rushed back, flushing her face with color. "It's none of your damned business whether or not I'm—!"

"It's my business if I'm the father! Or won't you be able to tell who the father is?" he asked nastily.

Lucy swung at him, only to have him grab her wrist and hold it away from her body. As strong as she was, she was no match for Stone's wiry strength.

Trembling with anger, she glared at him, willing herself not to cry, not to look away, not to give an inch. Pride wouldn't let her kick him, although she could have done him considerable damage with one well-placed blow, and they both knew it.

It was a battle of wills. A battle of . . .

She didn't know what else it was, but she did know that her emotions were wildly out of control, and she was beginning to suspect that his were, too.

"Let me go, Stone," she said quietly.

He did. She rubbed her wrist, but held her ground, unwilling to give him the satisfaction of seeing her run away.

"I still want to know if you're all right—and I don't mean what you think I mean, Lucy. There's more to it than that."

"Oh?" She was proud that her voice was steady, because she felt anything but steady inside. "What else do you think there is? I assure you, I don't—"

"Dammit, if I knew, I wouldn't be asking all these fool questions! I don't know what it means, but I do know what happened between us was more than just casual sex! You know it, too, only you're too damned stubborn to admit it!"

Lucy's heart was pounding so hard she could actually hear it. Dare she allow herself to hope that he felt it, too? Dare she risk *not* reaching out if there was the slightest chance that he cared? "Stone, are you trying to say that you love me?" she whispered.

"I'm not trying to say anything! I—" He broke off and swore, his face redder than it had been the night she had given him the tea bath.

I didn't say that. I couldn't *have said that!* Lucy closed her eyes while her world imploded in on her. She managed to stand her ground, but it was all she could do not to crawl under the nearest piece of furniture.

Stone's voice dropped half an octave, sounding rough as broken concrete. "Lucy, there's something you don't know."

The raw sound that emerged from her throat was meant to be laughter, but it fell far short of the mark. "You're married, right? And you're afraid that I'll—"

"No, dammit, I'm not married! It's nothing like that, only I have to tell you—"

"You don't have to tell me anything." She crossed her arms over her chest and stood her ground, wanting only to escape, to get as far away as possible. "I know what you're trying to say, Stone, and believe me, I understand."

"You don't understand one damned thing! There's no way you can underst—"

But she wouldn't let him finish. It was imperative that she speak her piece and get away before she embarrassed them both by bursting into tears. If she started crying now, it would ruin everything. "Stone, listen to me. I'm not a child. I know—well, I do know how these things can happen. All chemistry and no substance." God, that sounded like something she might tell her adolescent girls! "You know what the old song says about being too hot not to burn out." She attempted a laugh, but her voice broke, so she swallowed hard and went on, knowing that whatever she had to say, it was now or never.

And never was a long, long time to regret words not spoken.

"I want you to know," she began in a tremulous voice, "that whatever happened, I don't regret it and I don't expect—"

The door across the room swung back to clatter against the paneled wall. "Hey, Stone, come out here a minute, will you? Branscomb was telling us about this guy Hardisson who's running for state senate down in Georgia— something on the news last night about a scandal that's got the whole party down there up in arms, but he wasn't sure of the details. I told him I thought you two were related, so come give us the lowdown, okay? You're originally from that area, aren't you? I understand this guy's family is pretty big in politics down in that neck of the woods."

Ten

Stone and the Hardissons?

Somehow, Lucy got through the rest of the evening. By barricading herself behind the three children and beginning a rambling, extemporaneous tale about pirates and owls and three courageous, ingenious children who just happened to bear a striking resemblance to the Branscomb children, she managed not to hear anything more about Billy and his scandal and his possible relationship with Stone McCloud.

Stone and Billy?

Impossible. It was too big a coincidence, even for someone who habitually read her daily horoscope in the paper, and who never quite dared scoff at fate.

She was a Pisces, wasn't she? Pisces *believed*. Even Pisces with a home-loving, nest-building Cancer moon and a whole lot of earthy Taurus for balance. Lillian, who had dabbled in astrology, had told her all about

herself—her strengths, weaknesses and conflicts—and
about all the searching she would have to do before she
could ever hope to find true fulfillment. She had also told
her that once she found true fulfillment—or true fulfillment found *her*—she would recognize it in the very bones
of her soul.

So much for true fulfillment.

Stone hung around until nearly ten. Too often for
comfort she felt his gaze on her, but he stayed with the
men and she stayed with the women and children. It was
that kind of a party.

The Branscombs finally left to bed down their brood.
Lucy insisted on doing most of the cleanup, and Maudie,
sensing—if not understanding—her need to stay busy,
didn't argue.

Drat the man, why didn't he go home! Lucy knew, as
surely as she knew anything, that he was waiting for her
to leave, and the minute she did, he'd be right behind her.

And she wasn't ready to talk to him now. She didn't
want to know about his connection with Billy.

Correction. She was *afraid* to know.

Forty-five minutes later, Lucy gave up. The Mirandas
had left shortly after the Branscombs, Reece had said
good-night even before that, and Maudie was beginning
to yawn quite pointedly.

"I guess I'd better get on back to the cottage," Lucy
said reluctantly.

"Want to borrow a flashlight?"

"Thanks, but the moon—"

"I'll see her home," said Stone, who had come up silently behind her. There was little she could do without
making a scene. Tight-lipped, she collected her salad
bowl from the kitchen and thanked them both for a

lovely evening. Then, scowling at Stone, she stalked out the door.

Moonlight cast a nacreous glow over everything, deepening the shadows of the woods. A chorus of tree frogs almost, but not quite, drowned out the deeper notes of the bullfrogs and a haunting duet by a pair of chuck-will's-widows.

Lucy paused only a moment to get her bearings. Then, breathing in the warm, salt-tinged fragrance of the night, she set off down the barely visible sand path at a brisk pace.

"You don't have to run. I'm not going to attack you on the way home," Stone said, dry amusement coloring his voice.

"It never occurred to me that you were," she flung over her shoulders.

"Then why've you been avoiding me all night?"

"Avoiding you?" God, was that flimsy little voice hers?

"Knock it off, Lucy. Sooner or later we're going to have to talk about it."

Three steps ahead of him, she stopped suddenly and turned to confront him. "All right, you want to talk about something? Then how about talking about you and Billy! How about telling me who you really are and what you're doing here, because I know damned well you're not down here for the bird-watching! You couldn't tell a sea gull from a sardine if your life depended on it!"

Grasping her by the arm, Stone steered her toward cottage row, pulling ahead as his own anger outstripped hers. His was directed toward himself, which didn't make it any easier to bear.

No, dammit! He was mad as hell, all right, but it wasn't at himself, and it certainly wasn't at Lucy!

They reached her cottage first, and as tempted as Stone was to force his way in, to settle the most important matters before things got any messier than they already were, common sense prevailed.

"Look, I don't want to leave you like this," he said gruffly.

"Then I'll leave you. I don't mind at all."

But she was all eaten up inside. He could tell from the way she held herself, as if she was afraid of falling apart. He could tell by the brittleness of her voice, which was usually so soft and husky. She could be forceful, all right—she could spit it out like a drill sergeant when she was of a mind to—but she wasn't being forceful now. She was being . . .

Ah, sweet Jesus, how could he have been so blind?

"Lucy, listen, I—"

"No. I don't want to hear it. Whatever you're up to, I don't want to know anything about it. You lied to me, and—"

"I did not *lie* to you!"

"No?" she asked coolly, her arms wrapped tightly around her chest as if it were a cold night in January instead of a hot, humid night in midsummer.

"Okay, so maybe—maybe I didn't exactly level with you right up front, but if you'll let me explain, you'll understand why—"

"You don't need to explain anything. If you came down here looking to pick up Billy's leavings, you succeeded. I hope you both have a good laugh—it must have been quite a joke. Only, you'll excuse me if I don't think it's very funny."

Before she could turn away, Stone reached out and pulled her into his arms, elbows and all. It was not a comfortable embrace, and when he tried to kiss her, she came down hard on his left foot with her right one. His mouth skittered across her cheek, and not until she had stalked into the house, slammed the door and then hooked it behind her, did he realize his own face was wet.

Wet from her tears. She'd been crying. His big, beautiful, sweet, sweet Lucy—his tough-as-nails, soft-as-a-marshmallow Lucy.

The woman who thought Alice Hardisson was a kind, generous lady, a friend who had done her a big favor.

God, what a crock!

Swearing under his breath, Stone churned the few hundred feet through the powdery sand, still warm with the heat of the sun, to his own cottage. A few feet from the door, he was suddenly struck by a blast of heavy metal.

Great. That was all he needed. Evidently, Reece had collected his boom box from the trunk of his car when he'd gone over to shop for groceries. As mood music went, Stone had to admit that it was right on target.

Lucy was gone by the time Stone woke up the next morning. He checked by the Keegans' place, but she wasn't there. She wasn't at her usual swimming hole, and all the boats were tied up at the pier.

Just in case she was sulking, he'd banged on both doors of her cottage and called through the windows. Not that he'd expected her to throw out the welcome mat. Still, he would have thought that after a night's sleeping, she might have been willing to give him the benefit of the doubt. Wasn't she even curious about his connection with the Hardissons, and what he was doing here on Coronoke?

He wanted to tell her. He *needed* to tell her! But, dammit, if she was going to play hide-and-seek, she was just going to have to play it alone, because he had other fish to fry.

Alice, for a start. That woman owed him a few answers, and he was going to get them. After he'd finished with his aunt, he was going to start in on Billy, because Billy was at the root of the whole damned mess.

But first, Alice. Eyeball to eyeball, on account of his aunt had a bad habit of speaking her piece on the phone and hanging up without giving her opponent a chance to fire a single shot.

He made arrangements with a guy named Dwight to fly him to Norfolk from Billy Mitchell Airport over on Hatteras. Next he called Norfolk International and made reservations on the first flight out to Atlanta, after which he told Reece to close up the cottage if it looked like rain. "Sorry about this, man—something came up at the last minute. You know how it is in this business."

"Yeah, sure—no sweat. Anything you want me to tell Lucy for you? Like how long you'll be gone, or where you're going?" He waited expectantly, his good-looking face wide open for the reading, and it occurred to Stone that the ploy just might work to his advantage one of these days.

But not on Stone. Not on a pro. "Better learn to play 'em a little closer to your vest, son. You'll stand a better chance of getting what you're after." Then, his eyes taking on the steely sheen of still waters under a stormy sky, he said, "Tell her I'm going after the answers to all the questions she should have asked and didn't."

"Huh?"

"Just tell her that, will you?"

"If you say so. Uh—Stone, can I have the last of the potato salad, or will you be wanting it for supper?"

"Clean out the refrigerator and we'll start over. I'll stop by the deli on my way back tomorrow. And Reece— keep an eye on her for me, will you?"

His answer was a broad grin and a double thumbs-up.

It was all over the papers. Stone picked up a couple at the airport in Norfolk while he waited for his flight to be called. The story made page two in the *Ledger-Dispatch,* page three in the *News and Observer.* Two hours later, he picked up a *Constitution* at Hartsfield outside the car rental agency and stopped to scan the headlines. He didn't have to look beyond page one. Local Candidate Accused Of Sexual Harassment. According to the pull-quote, several women's groups were demanding Hardisson's scalp.

So what else was new?

Traffic was bumper to bumper. Horns blared. The air inside the car reeked of new vinyl and stale perfume. Outside was no better. Hot dust, exhaust fumes and burning rubber. He'd picked a hell of a time to tackle Atlanta. Or Atlanna, as his aunt called it.

Stone swore, sweated and swore some more. He thought about a small, quiet island that smelled of salt marsh and maritime forest. He thought about floating on an inner tube under a clear, pollution-free sky. He thought about a certain big, beautiful, slow-talking, slow-smiling, brown-eyed blonde.

From the next lane over, a horn blasted. A kid in a red Trans Am flipped him a one-finger salute, scratched off, and he swore again.

"Miz Hardisson's not in," said the maid. She started to close the door, and then looked at him more closely. "My lawsy, aren't you—"

"Her nephew, that's right. And you're Rosalie."

The elderly woman in the gray-and-white uniform beamed. "Can't believe you remembered me after all these years, Mr. John. Come on in. I reckon seein's how you're family, Miz Alice'll want to visit with you. You go on into the sun parlor, and I'll just go tell her you're here. She's been feelin' right puny lately, what with all this ruckus we been havin'. Got so for a few days we couldn't open the front door 'thout steppin' all over folks from the newspaper and the television. Worse'n June bugs swarmin' on a muscadine vine!"

Stone spent more than an hour with his aunt. He'd gone in fully intending to nail her to the wall, but in the end, he'd relented. She looked like hell. He got part of the story from her, part from the local news channel and some from old Liam, whom he tracked down with the help of Rosalie, who'd been only a maid when he'd lived there, but who was now the Hardisson's housekeeper.

"I'm not gonna tell you no more'n that, Mr. John, on account of I like my job too much," the woman had said when she saw him to the front door. "I'll just say this much. It's been real hard on Miz Alice. She tried her best with that boy, but it never done a speck o' good. Too easy on him, if you ask me. She should've put 'er foot down the first time he rared up to her. If he was mine, I'd have tanned his britches for him, but Miz Alice don't like to raise her voice. Never did, more's the pity."

"You think there's anything to this latest story?"

"About all them women comin' out o' the woodwork, a-claimin' he done all those awful things to 'em? Wouldn't surprise me none. I remember how he used to treat that little dog o' Miz Alice's when she weren't lookin'."

Stone remembered, too. He remembered the day he'd found the poor wretch and buried it, and told his aunt that it had run out in the street and gotten hit by a car. "I guess you knew his wife?"

"Miz Lucy? I knew 'er. Billy weren't good enough to lick the dirt off'n the soles o' her shoes. He told some awful tales about her after she run off, but I knew *her* an' I know *him*. I got a pretty good idea what happened, an' it's not what he tried to make folks believe. You go tell Liam I said he was to tell you about all the times that girl didn't dare show her poor face around town. Couldn't even cover up the bruises, poor baby, on account o' powder and paint made her break out somethin' awful. Get Liam to tell you about that last time she went to the emergency room, when Miz Alice was off on one o' her trips. Miz Lucy tried to keep it to herself on account o' she didn't want to hurt Miz Alice's feelin's, but my second cousin on the Sutphin side o' the family works at the hospital in records, and she told me things that just about broke my heart. I never said a word to Miz Alice, though. It'd kill her, sure's the world."

Stone felt cold inside. He didn't really want to hear any more. He'd already heard too much. "Thanks, Rosalie. Take care of Aunt Alice, will you? She needs all the friends she can get." *Damn her blind, meddling soul!*

"I'll do that, Mr. John. Now you wait right here a minute while I fetch a bottle o' Miz Alice's best sippin' whiskey. She'll never miss it, and old Liam needs it for his joints. It's about all that keeps him goin' these days."

Stone got a late flight out of Hartsfield, having arranged for a charter to fly him from Norfolk to Hatteras. If the trip south had seemed endless, the dogleg trip back to Coronoke wasn't nearly long enough. Not long enough to assimilate everything he had learned, nor long enough to figure out how much of it he was going to tell Lucy.

If she was still there. He should have told Reece to sit on her if he had to, but not to let her leave the island. No damned wonder the woman was skittish! First that father of hers, dragging her from pillar to post, leaving her to the tender mercies of whichever woman he happened to be sleeping with at the time.

And then she'd had the rotten luck to get mixed up with Bill Hardisson, user and abuser of women, alcohol and drugs. A man with enough surface charm, family clout and money to get by with murder!

Or close enough.

But not any longer. Two weeks before his much publicized wedding to the daughter of a highly respectable member of the clergy, one of his past victims had sold a sordid little tale to a gossip sheet, and that had primed the pump. Three more women had come forth, and the media had a field day. This time, neither the Hardisson money nor the Hardisson charm could manage to gloss over the deficiency in the Hardisson character. Billy's political career might eventually recover. In politics, character didn't seem to matter a lot these days. However, Alice probably wouldn't recover. Stone found it in his heart to feel sorry for her, even if he couldn't forgive what she had tried to do to Lucy.

Lucy. He was going to have to tell her—some of it, at least.

Stone sighed. He wasn't looking forward to it.

Eleven

Funny thing about time, Stone mused tiredly as he set off on the last leg of his trip. Over the past two days—and more than a thousand miles—time had alternately raced by at phenomenal speeds or crawled like a snail on gravel. Heading south, dreading what he would discover, he'd found time rushing to meet him. On the way back to Coronoke, it had dragged interminably while he sweated out every mile, wondering whether or not Lucy would still be there, whether or not she would listen to his explanations. And exactly what he was going to say to her once he convinced her to hear him out.

He was still shaken by the feeling that he had just relived his entire lifetime in the space of less than forty-eight hours. Atlanta had changed almost beyond recognition in the years since he had left his aunt's Buckhead mansion at the age of fourteen, but some things remained the same. Fortunately, he still had a couple of contacts at police headquarters, another one in county records—not to mention a few friends in the local press. He'd made good use of them all.

And Liam. Old, bent, with his hair—what there was of it—completely white now. But that rusty laugh of his hadn't changed, nor had the wisdom and the gentleness that had pulled a lost kid through some pretty rough times.

And Rosalie, all two hundred-odd pounds of her, God bless her big heart, her stubborn loyalty and her outspoken ways.

Stone made the skiff fast and stepped up onto the pier, slinging his overnight bag ahead of him. Back on the familiar sandy shore, he paused to gaze up the slight incline toward the dense, vine-hung, wind-sculpted forest. Against the darkness stood a single bleached ghost of long-dead cedar, holding a lonely vigil against the encroaching waters.

The quietness was suddenly broken by a hoarse croak—either a frog or a heron. He didn't know which, and what was more, he didn't give a sweet damn. He was back. Back in Camelot. Back on Coronoke, where nothing really changed but the seasons and the weather, and even those were familiar friends, leaving only to come again.

She had to be here. She damn well *had* to be here, because if she was gone, Stone would have felt it in his bones the minute he stepped ashore. And if thoughts like that meant he had finally lost it, then so be it.

Just so he hadn't lost his Lucy.

Lucy was helping Maudie strip her finished canvases, using quarter-inch-thick lattice strips painted white, tacking them directly onto the canvas stretchers. The result was a finished look for a fraction of the cost of a frame.

"Here, this is the last one. Hand me those cutting pliers, will you?" Maudie was attaching screw eyes and wire to each painting, ready for hanging. "How do you like the yellow skiff against the marsh?"

"I like it. But why not red, like your boat? I don't think I've ever seen a yellow one, come to think of it."

"Yellow works better. Poetic license isn't only for poets."

Lucy smiled. A few days ago, she might even have laughed, but nothing seemed funny anymore. Nor even faintly amusing.

"He'll be back, you know," Maudie said gently. It was as close as either of them had come to mentioning Stone McCloud.

Lucy shrugged and laid aside her tack hammer to prop the finished canvas against the wall with the others. "You ever have one-woman shows?"

"I've had a few. I hate watching people look at my work, though. It's like standing there naked as a newborn baby, inviting people to throw stones. Besides, it's only tourist art."

"Honestly!" Shaking her head at her friend's modesty, Lucy cranked the handle on the side of the old Victrola again. While they worked, they'd been listening to a collection of old Jimmie Rodgers 78s left over from the days when Rich's grandfather had maintained a hunt club on the island. When the last song ended, Maudie tilted her head.

"I thought I heard a plane a few minutes ago."

"You heard a freight train." They had just played "Brakeman's Blues."

"Not down here, I didn't. Did I tell you I saw Dwight at the post office? He said he was supposed to pick up a fare at Norfolk today and fly him back to Billy Mitchell. Three guesses who it is."

To her acute dismay, Lucy felt her face begin to burn. "So?" she muttered defensively.

Maudie's green eyes glistened wickedly. "So—what are you waiting for? Get on home and hop in the tub. Scrub the paint off your hands, douse yourself with something seductive and put on your sexiest outfit."

"I don't own a sexy outfit. And if I douse myself with anything stronger than unscented soap, I'll look like a boiled-hard crab. And anyhow, I—"

"Don't argue, woman, just go. *Go!*"

Lucy went. She was still in her bathtub when she heard the sound of an outboard motor. It wasn't Stone—it couldn't be Stone—and even if it was, there was no reason to think he'd come back to see her. Reece had said—

Reece had said a lot of things, most of which Lucy had dismissed as his creative imagination. She had enough trouble with her own imagination, without adding his to the pot.

Stone's leaving had nothing to do with her. His returning—if he did—would have nothing to do with her, either. To believe otherwise would be asking for more heartache than she was equipped to handle. Lucy knew about heartache. She could see it coming a mile away, and she had promised herself—she really had—that she would never again hang around for a closer look.

So much for promises.

"Lucy!" Someone rattled her screen door and she froze, one foot in the iron-stained bathtub, one foot on the soft yellow bath mat.

"Dammit, Lucy, I know you're in there, so open up!"

"I'm not home," she yelled, clutching a towel in front of her. As a sop to her modesty, it was barely adequate.

"Look, I'm too tired to play games. Dammit, would you just open this door! Please?"

The silence was broken only by the soft *peep-peep* of an osprey.

"Lucy, I'm warning you—"

"Stone, I don't feel like company. If you have anything to say, you can say it tomorrow."

"Dammit, it's your screen door, you can pay the damages."

A moment later he was scowling at her from the bathroom doorway, looking pale, tired, rumpled and unshaven. "Sorry—I didn't mean to barge in on you this way."

"Oh? You mean it was purely unintentional, your tearing loose my screen door and forcing your way into my house?" She was so furious, she was shaking all over.

Which had to be the reason her voice was trembling like a leaf in a hurricane. For one brief moment, she thought he looked stricken with guilt, but it was probably just her imagination. "Turn your back," she growled, and he did.

But he didn't leave. Not right away. "For God's sake, put something on!"

"Get out."

"Lucy, we've got to sort this mess out!"

"There's nothing to sort."

"Do you have to be so goddamned independent all the time?" Stone demanded. His shoulders were hunched, his fists rammed into his pockets. Lucy stared at his back, at the worn jeans that clung to his narrow hips and hard calves, skimming everything in between, at the shaggy dark hair that barely grazed the collar of his faded khaki shirt. It was all she could do not to reach out to him.

"All right, then I'll talk and you listen. I saw Alice. I spoke to Liam and Rosalie. They sent you their love, by the way—that is, Liam and Rosalie did."

Lucy knew when she was licked. "Go sit down in the living room, Stone. I'll be out in a minute," she said quietly. Whatever he had to say, he was determined she was going to hear. So be it. Maybe then she could close the cover on this brief chapter of her life and get on with the next.

Nine minutes later, when she emerged from the bedroom, Stone was sprawled across her sofa, snoring softly. Uttering a small sound of defeat, Lucy moved to stand over him, so close she could feel the heat from his body— see the crow's-feet fanned out at the corners of his eyes. There was a faint white line on the underside of his jaw that she hadn't noticed before.

Another scar. They both had them, visible and invisible. Maybe everyone did. Life was a scary place, if you let it be.

And then he was awake. He didn't move a muscle. One instant he was breathing deeply, evenly, and the next moment he was lying there like a wary jungle animal, watching her. Waiting to see which way she was going to jump. If he'd had a tail, it would've been twitching.

She jumped in the safest direction. "Do you want something to eat? I made a double batch of spaghetti, thinking Reece would share it, but he left this morning. Something about a girl in Carrboro, I think."

They ate cold spaghetti with half a pound of cheddar grated over the top. Stone claimed he preferred it cold. As far as Lucy was concerned, caviar and the sturgeon it came in, dressed with every sauce in the book, would

have been utterly wasted. She ate because it was something to do with her mouth besides talking.

But not even a big girl with a big appetite could eat
forever.

"You wash, I'll dry," Stone offered after polishing off
two platefuls of the cold pasta with a diet cola, which was
all she'd had to offer.

But in the end, they left the dishes where they were.
There were too many silent questions hanging in the air.
Questions that demanded answers. And Lucy was beginning to feel queasy. Nerves and cold spaghetti didn't
mix too well.

The screened porch was mercifully dark, with only a
single light from the kitchen falling across the worn
decking, but that was more than enough for Lucy to notice that Stone was edgy. He leaned forward, resting his
forearms on his thighs. Then he sighed and leaned back
again. "I guess you know I went to Atlanta."

"Reece said something about an assignment. That
wasn't it, was it?"

"No, it wasn't about an assignment—or maybe it was.
It was about you. About you and Billy—and Alice. She's
my aunt, although we've never been close—which makes
Billy my first cousin."

Suddenly, the night didn't feel nearly as warm, nearly
as safe. "I don't understand."

There was a quiet dignity about her that threatened to
tear Stone apart. "I've got a lot of apologizing to do,
Lucy. I'd appreciate it if you'd let me get through that
much, at least, without interrupting. After that, the
floor's yours."

For a man who made his living with words, Stone
found himself damned near inarticulate. After several
false starts, during which she sat there like a queen giv-

ing audience to a beggar, he blurted out the whole sorry business from beginning to end, including what he'd learned from family and from his own private sources. He felt sick all over again, thinking about what the bastards had put her through—and then, on top of all that, how they'd lied about her to make it sound as if the rumors that were beginning to circulate had been deliberately stirred up by a greedy, irate ex-wife looking to cash in with a timely little spot of blackmail.

Several minutes passed in silence after he'd finally run down. And then she said carefully, "So all along you've only been wanting to trap me into—"

"No, dammit! I never wanted to trap you into anything!"

"All right, then you wanted to keep me from stirring up trouble. And there was no companion with a broken hip. It was all a lie. The cottage that would have gone to waste if I didn't take it. Your bird-watching. Mother—that is, Mrs. Hardisson's—"

Her voice threatened to break, and Stone swore silently. Somewhere between Atlanta and Coronoke he had reluctantly forgiven his aunt for sticking up for her son. Mothers were occasionally prone to selective blindness. But he could never forgive her for the ruthless way she had used Lucy, who had, in spite of everything, still thought Mother Hardisson had hung the moon.

So much for noblesse oblige. "Lucy, listen to me—I know this whole affair started out all wrong, but that part's over. There's no reason to waste what we've found."

From a seated position, she grew visibly taller. A new moon, just lifting above the treetops, haloed her crop of pale curls and glistened on something wet on her right cheek.

Stone felt a fist begin to tighten around his heart. He had flat run out of words, and words weren't what mattered now, anyhow. Before she could protest, he was beside her, drawing her stiff body into his arms. "I'll make it up to you—if it takes a lifetime, I promise, I'll make it all up to you, Lucy. What they've done, what I did—"

As his words were interspersed with small kisses, it took a while to make the promise, and even then he couldn't be sure she understood what he was trying to say.

Standing, he drew her up into the circle of his arms. She neither resisted nor cooperated. "It doesn't matter," she said dully. "Anyway, it's all in the past." Tomorrow—or maybe the day after—she would have to pack up and leave.

Gently, as if to awaken her, Stone shook her. "But what about the future?"

She was so tired. Briefly she rested her head on his shoulder.

The future? "Nothing's changed," she said. Everything's changed, a voice screamed inside her. "I still have my job. I still have a place to live. I still have my friends. I still have my—"

My dreams?

Her face crumpled. A small sob escaped her, and she mumbled an apology for being such a wimp, and Stone muttered some maudlin nonsense that should have embarrassed the hell out of him, but didn't. "Come here. Let me wash your face, sugar," he said gruffly, leading her inside past the merciless glare of the kitchen light and into the bathroom. "If I had any magic recipes, like tea baths or baking soda, I'd trot 'em out, but I'm afraid I'm not much good at home remedies. Here—blow your nose, darling."

Half laughing, half sobbing, Lucy took the tissue he offered and blew. She was too tired to resist any longer. Leaning over the basin, she splashed cold water over her face, praying it would disguise any blotchiness around her eyes. Somehow, it didn't even strike her as strange to be sharing her bathroom with a man she had never laid eyes upon a few weeks ago.

But then, she'd shared far more than a bathroom with him.

"You got water all over your pretty pink shirt," Stone pointed out, his voice a tender rumble in his throat. "That's all you need now, to catch a cold."

"Colds come from germs. Or viruses—I'm not sure which," she said with a broken laugh.

"Don't discount the effects of lowered resistance."

"Stone, why don't you go home? You've said what you came to say, and—"

"As it happens," he interrupted, "I do know a thing or two about lowered resistance. For instance, there's nothing like bed rest to ward off all kinds of nasty germs."

"For pity sakes, I'm not worried about germs! I'm not worried about catching cold. I'm not—"

"What are you worried about, Lucy?"

She made a noise in her throat that, roughly translated, meant, *I don't believe this!* "Thanks for your concern, but it's a bit too late. If you'd never listened to Alice, if I'd had the brains to look a gift horse in the mouth, if I'd settled for a weekend at Busch Gardens with Frank and the children instead of walking blindly into a trap, if I'd—"

"Who's Frank? What children?"

"Never mind, it doesn't matter now."

"Lucy?" With a thumb under her chin, Stone tilted her face up to his. He searched her eyes, ignoring their faint pinkness, ignoring the accusations he saw there—or maybe he only imagined them. God knows he deserved them. "Lucy, you didn't let me finish. I don't know if it matters or not, but I never got around to telling you that I, uh—I love you."

Thumb or no thumb, Lucy's jaw dropped. "Don't do this to me, Stone."

"Why not? You've done it to me."

"I haven't done one blessed thing to you. What happened the other night was only an—"

"An accident? Don't hand me that, lady, because I know better."

"You don't know—"

"Don't I?" His hands held her arms in a loose, unbreakable grip. Silently, he challenged her to look him in the eye.

Lucy could never refuse a dare. It was one of her failings. One of her many failings. She lifted her gaze a few inches, and that was her first mistake. Her second, staring into those clear gray eyes of his, was trying to convince herself that every cell of her body wasn't aching for him. That the thought of never seeing him again—never loving him again—wasn't destroying her.

"You love me, too," he said, barely above a whisper. Heat flared in his eyes, and he said triumphantly, "You do! Say it, Lucy. Tell me! I need to hear the words."

"Why? So that you can go back and compare notes with Billy?"

Before the words were even out, she regretted them. "Stone, that wasn't me talking—I didn't really mean that. I know you would never do something like that."

She saw the pain in his eyes, and it nearly killed her. "Stone, please—I'm sorry. Say something!"

His voice sounding as if it had been strained through burlap, he said, "Billy admitted that he married you because it was the only way he could have you. Billy's always wanted what he couldn't have."

She started to speak, but he laid a finger over her lips. "Hear me out. Lucy, I love you. I care more about you than I've ever cared for another soul, in ways I can't even begin to describe. If the choice is between having you forever or sleeping with you now, I'll take forever. Do you understand what I'm saying?"

Her heart swelling painfully, Lucy reached up and insinuated her hands under his. Stepping back, she led him from the bathroom into her bedroom. Not a word was spoken until she stood beside the bed. Then, turning, she said, "There's a third choice." She began unbuttoning his shirt, and Stone watched her fingers, scarcely daring to breathe.

By the time she got to his pants, unbuckling his belt, unsnapping the top of his fly, breathing wasn't even a consideration. Spontaneous combustion was a definite possibility. "Lucy," he said hoarsely. "Sweetheart, if this is some kind of twisted revenge, consider it done."

She started in on her own shirt, which was still wet from its recent splashing. "I told you once, I've never been very good at games. Stone, I want you to make love to me, and if—if you still want to marry me, then I want it, too."

There was no more waiting. Stone's hands were shaking so bad he jammed his zipper and Lucy had to work it loose. Which nearly killed him. Once his clothes were on the floor, she tore off her own, dropping them in a pile to stand before him naked and unashamed. She trusted him. She wanted him. She loved him. It was that simple.

The night could have lasted forever, and it wouldn't have been long enough for Lucy. In his arms, she came apart again and again as he took her to places she had never dreamed of before. "Touch me here—touch me there" became "Kiss me here—kiss me there."

He kissed the soles of her feet, tickling her arch, suckling her toes, and then explored his way up the long, satiny length of her legs. He told her about the thoughts that had passed through his mind on first seeing her—about what he'd wanted to do to her even then.

And then he did it.

Lucy, free at last of the echoes of Lillian's strictures and warnings, of Billy's cruel remarks and comparisons, soared to the heavens. She gave of herself freely, and took just as freely, and Stone gloried in it.

"You've got to be too tired for this," she said once, her soft halo of curls tickling the scar of his lower belly. "You've been traveling for two days."

Stone stiffened as her mouth brushed against him. If her hands were magic, her mouth was indescribable. "I've been— Ah, precious, *yes!*" He groaned, and then tried again. "I've been traveling for years, only I never knew why. Now that I've finally found you, I'm going to have to figure out some way to stay home, because—"

"Or I could go with you. I'm a good traveler." She moved up over his body, on her knees and elbows, to stare gravely into his face.

Stone had a feeling if she'd asked him to bury himself in a hole in the ground for the next millennium, he'd have grabbed a shovel and started digging. "I've been thinking about finding a small town somewhere and putting down a few roots. I've had this offer, and—well, a man can't keep up this pace forever."

Lucy chuckled. "Oh, I don't know . . . for a man your age in your condition, you're not doing bad at all."

She was on her back in an instant, with Stone leaning over her, a dangerous glint in his eyes. "We'll talk about how well a man my age can do when I hit fifty. And again at sixty, and about every decade after that. Meanwhile . . ."

* * * * *

IT'S OUR 1000TH SILHOUETTE ROMANCE, AND WE'RE CELEBRATING!

JOIN US FOR A SPECIAL COLLECTION OF LOVE STORIES
BY AUTHORS YOU'VE LOVED FOR YEARS, AND
NEW FAVORITES YOU'VE JUST DISCOVERED.
JOIN THE CELEBRATION...

April
REGAN'S PRIDE by Diana Palmer
MARRY ME AGAIN by Suzanne Carey

May
THE BEST IS YET TO BE by Tracy Sinclair
CAUTION: BABY AHEAD by Marie Ferrarella

June
THE BACHELOR PRINCE by Debbie Macomber
A ROGUE'S HEART by Laurie Paige

July
IMPROMPTU BRIDE by Annette Broadrick
THE FORGOTTEN HUSBAND by Elizabeth August

SILHOUETTE ROMANCE...VIBRANT, FUN AND EMOTIONALLY
RICH! TAKE ANOTHER LOOK AT US! AND AS PART OF THE
CELEBRATION, READERS CAN RECEIVE A FREE GIFT!

YOU'LL FALL IN LOVE ALL OVER
AGAIN WITH
SILHOUETTE ROMANCE!

Silhouette®

CEL1000

MILLION DOLLAR SWEEPSTAKES (III)

No purchase necessary. To enter, follow the directions published. Method of entry may vary. For eligibility, entries must be received no later than March 31, 1996. No liability is assumed for printing errors, lost, late or misdirected entries. Odds of winning are determined by the number of eligible entries distributed and received. Prizewinners will be determined no later than June 30, 1996.

Sweepstakes open to residents of the U.S. (except Puerto Rico), Canada, Europe and Taiwan who are 18 years of age or older. All applicable laws and regulations apply. Sweepstakes offer void wherever prohibited by law. Values of all prizes are in U.S. currency. This sweepstakes is presented by Torstar Corp., its subsidiaries and affiliates, in conjunction with book, merchandise and/or product offerings. For a copy of the Official Rules send a self-addressed, stamped envelope (WA residents need not affix return postage) to: MILLION DOLLAR SWEEPSTAKES (III) Rules, P.O. Box 4573, Blair, NE 68009, USA.

EXTRA BONUS PRIZE DRAWING

No purchase necessary. The Extra Bonus Prize will be awarded in a random drawing to be conducted no later than 5/30/96 from among all entries received. To qualify, entries must be received by 3/31/96 and comply with published directions. Drawing open to residents of the U.S. (except Puerto Rico), Canada, Europe and Taiwan who are 18 years of age or older. All applicable laws and regulations apply; offer void wherever prohibited by law. Odds of winning are dependent upon number of eligibile entries received. Prize is valued in U.S. currency. The offer is presented by Torstar Corp., its subsidiaries and affiliates in conjunction with book, merchandise and/or product offering. For a copy of the Official Rules governing this sweepstakes, send a self-addressed, stamped envelope (WA residents need not affix return postage) to: Extra Bonus Prize Drawing Rules, P.O. Box 4590, Blair, NE 68009, USA.

SWP-S594

CAN YOU STAND THE HEAT?

SUMMER Sizzlers '94

You're in for a serious heat wave with Silhouette's latest selection of sizzling summer reading. This sensuous collection of three short stories provides the perfect vacation escape! And what better authors to relax with than

ANNETTE BROADRICK
JACKIE MERRITT
JUSTINE DAVIS

And that's not all....

With the purchase of *Silhouette Summer Sizzlers '94*, you can send in for a FREE Summer Sizzlers beach bag!

SUMMER JUST GOT HOTTER— WITH SILHOUETTE BOOKS!

Rugged and lean...and the best-looking, sweetest-talking men to be found in the entire Lone Star state!

In July 1994, Silhouette is very proud to bring you Diana Palmer's first three LONG, TALL TEXANS. CALHOUN, JUSTIN and TYLER—the three cowboys who started the legend. Now they're back by popular demand in one classic volume—and they're ready to lasso your heart! Beautifully repackaged for this special event, this collection is sure to be a longtime keepsake!

"Diana Palmer makes a reader want to find a Texan of her own to love!" —*Affaire de Coeur*

LONG, TALL TEXANS—the first three—reunited in this special roundup!

**Available in July,
wherever Silhouette books are sold.**